Consciously Barefoot

CONSCIOUSLY BAREFOOT
- About Earthing and healing inflammations
ISBN 9781692541842

Copyright © Lilian Alterskjaer 2018
Published in Sweden 2018 by Grön Kärlek Förlag
Original title: MEDVETET BARFOTA - Om jordning & att läka dina inflammationer

English edition © Lilian Alterskjaer 2019
Publisher: Grön Kärlek Förlag
Translator: Christina Maria Bladh

All rights reserved. The book may not be reproduced, reproduced or transmitted in any form or by any means, electronically or mechanically (including photocopying), recorded or stored in any form of information or retrieval program, without the publisher's written permission.

Cover design and illustrations: Jenny Holmlund
Photographs: Karin Sundemo
Content design: Renée Edlund, StjärnDistribution

Printed by Booksfactory, Polen 2019

www.gronkarlek.se
www.medvetetbarfota.se

CONSCIOUSLY BAREFOOT
– About Earthing and healing inflammations

Lilian Alterskjaer

**This book is dedicated to you,
my reader**

*My hope and wish are that the contents
of this book, will be the beginning
of something new and great for you!*

Lilian Alterskjaer

Content

This book you are reading 9
My wish with this book is to give you 11
My dream 13
My own story... 16

Part one – Consciously Barefoot
Chapter 1. Earthing/Grounding 22
To Ground yourself... 22
Why walk Barefoot, what happens?................... 23
No animals walk with shoes!............................. 24
Clint Ober 25
What does conduct material mean?................... 25
What is EMF?... 26
What can be damaging with EMF?..................... 27
Glossary 28

Chapter 2. Why should we Ground ourselves? 33
Health effects 33
Antioxidants 35
Chronic inflammation and electron deficiency........ 37
Medicine against aging 39
Pets and Earthing 39
Pregnant women, children and Earthing 40
Reduce pain... 41

Chapter 3. How to Ground yourself 43
Just go outside 43
Our magical feet 44
Walking and running Barefoot 45
Ocean and lakes give an electron bath 47
Earthing indoors 49

In the forest 50
Beloved thunder 51
**Chapter 4. Reduce and avoid EMP at home
and at work** 53
Are we being naive and blind? 53
How can we measure EMF? 54
Advice for a healthier indoor environment 62
How do I know what are grounded outlets
and cords? 64
Chapter 5. Electrons in cold climates 70
To be Grounded indoors 70
Health with machines and technical equipment 72
My own beloved machine 74
Chapter 6. Other aspects of the term Earthing 75

Part two – Conscious everyday Breathing
Chapter 7. Breathing 84
Conscious everyday Breathing 84
Cells, Breathing and Earthing 86
Close your mouth 90
There is only one thing to do! Breathe through
the nose! 91
Reduce inflammation 92
For weight hunters and athletes 93
Stressed, Burnout 94
Four good advice 95

Part three – Conscious nutrition
Chapter 8. Food 98
Food for the cells 98
The right fatty acid balance 100
Diseases that usually have their origin
in inflammation 105

What does chronic mean? 106
My own awakening 107
Choice of Omega-3 Oil 111
Why we should take Omega-3? 112
Some answers to the question "Why don't you
     want to be without the oil" 114
Advice...114
Find out if your "oil lamp" is on red or green! 115
The ruin of sugar 116
Intestinal bacteria and intestinal flora 117
Wild plants for food, spice and medicine 119
Find out your particular nutrition needs 121
Do a hair mineral analysis 123
You are your bedrock 124
Diet that suppresses inflammation 125
Inflammation Free Diet 126
IBS free diet without Foodmaps...................... 127
Ketogenic diet.. 128
The cell's recycling system – autophagy 129

Part four – Conscious choices

Chapter 9. Dare to choose your road 136
Create new patterns................................. 136
Help for change 138
Feeling of context 139

What will your next step be?.........................141
Can I help you?...................................... 144
Thanks 145
References and research studies 147
Inspiration 152

This book you are reading

This book you are reading is supposed to be a practical book to be inspired by. You will get advice and tools on how to create more health, energy and well-being in your life.

If you are curious on how to strengthen yourself in simple and natural ways, this book is for you.

This is a self-help book that wants to inspire you to act.

The book will be your key to free and unlimited access, to the healing antioxidants of the Earth.

During the years I have learned from trial and error, and these two principles have helped me a lot:

- To have an open mind
- Take what you can use and leave the rest

I've been inspired by many scientific facts and studies. Scientific "truths" are stated as facts, and what today is considered true can be proven wrong in the future. In the end of the book, in the chapter "References and research studies" you find research I refer to in every chapter of the book.

One might say that in this book I'm touching on the surface of some topics that are much more extensive. If you get curious and want to know more, I hope that the simple composition and content of this book, can inspire you the reader, to dig deeper in areas that have awoken your curiosity that you want to learn more about.

It is important that you understand that no information in my book is in any way meant to be medical guidance or claim to be a remedy for a medical disease. Always consult with a doctor regarding your personal health.

My wish with this book is to give you

- An understanding of why bare skin contact with the Earth is beneficial for your health. An introduction to Conscious Breathing and its benefits.

- An inspiration to choose the best diet, for your health and the cells in your body.

- A sense of how the interaction between Grounding, Consiously Breathing and food provides vitality.

- Tools to reduce inflammations that can be connected to illnesses.

- An insight into what the cells and mitochondria are doing for you

- A healthier life with better sleep, more energy, and less pain.

- More moments when you feel harmony and happiness.

- An insight into how radiation from electromagnetic fields (EMF) may be affecting you.

- Advice on how you can avoid and reduce your exposure to radiation and EMF.

My dream

My dream is to contribute to us human beings, the understanding of how to reclaim our relationship to ourselves and to Mother Nature. That we under the protective roof of the sky receive the support we need from nature, to our body's and soul's self-healing and development. I wish that my experiences, stories and scientific news and simple advice will grow some seeds in you, so you can easily choose your next steps, toward long-lasting health, happiness and freedom.

Being outside in Mother Nature has always been my favorite! In all shapes of engagement through the years that have passed, in one way or another I've contributed to get people, young and old, closer to nature. It is important to me that we all get a sense of belonging, how we are connected to Mother Earth and how we profoundly can respect each other. The more we understand how everything is connected, the more thankfulness and love will develop between us on Earth and Mother Nature. We are all a part of nature, yet sometimes we forget it.

The book is the result of many years of experimenting with everything from the Earth electrons to the healing power of wild plants. I've had periods in my life when both my health and my energy have not been good. In my search to rebuild myself I've found the answers in the most down to earth and simple ways, what is free for everyone to receive in nature.

I've learned so much from the people I've met: my parents, my relatives in Sweden and Norway, Saami, (the indigenous people of Sweden, Norway and Finland), hunters, farmers, healers, doctors, shamans, other writers, researchers, teachers and motivators. But the one that has meant the most, in my continued learning and researching is my dear friend Sussi. Oddly enough we have had almost identical challenges with our health. She brought up in Stockholm, five years younger than me with an academic education. Me, born in Sappetavan between two rivers in Vindelälven, in Northern part of Sweden near the Pole circle, and brought up on a self-sufficient farm, where we grew our food in the cleanest soil and raised farm animals. Despite heritage and environment being completely different, we have had the same question. How can we find natural keys to healing and health?

Could it be that we represent a big part of the Earth's population?

All the topics I touch upon, suggestions and advice that I give in this book, I tested myself.

I want to share what I have found, in the hope, that it will create health and development for you

My own story

I clearly remember how my Mom was angry with me every spring. It started already when the snow melted and the whole back yard at our home in Sappetavan was a delta of water channels. I dug in the ground to rearrange, to find new ways for the water to flow free and easy. A stone away there, a mess of leaves away over there. Of course, she was happy that I cleared up the water, that wasn't the problem. The problem was that I insisted on being Barefoot as soon as the snow melted, I considered it time to take off my shoes!

My attraction and strong bond with the Earth continued to grow. When I was young, I spent many years working as a dogsled driver, cabin host and waffle cook in the mountains, nature guide and taking care of reindeers together with Saami. To that life belonged, breaks during the workday with no shoes, fresh air in the lungs and branches and leaves from the birch tree in the tea. The health and wellbeing that I experienced was amazing! I had no colds, inflammations, or stomach problems!

One vivid memory, from those days, was when I lived in Ljungdalen, a little mountain village in Northern part of Sweden. It was the summer of 1985 if I remember correctly. The resourceful and active people of Ljungdalen had arranged a mountain marathon. I remember how I was at the finish line, and I was impressed by how the runners had ran through rocks, mud and tough mountain terrain for 42 kilometers and now reached the finish line with good speed. Among these power machines was the real tough guy, a man pushing fifty, running with a completely relaxed face, without shoes! The rumor said he had only eaten bananas. That man has been my role model ever since then! To run a marathon Barefoot, I have never tried, but walking Barefoot on the mountains or in the woods, that is like music in my heart and soul. When different material, temperatures, surfaces touch the soles of my feet, it sends signals to my whole body, I am alive! It is great! My favorite of them all, is walking Barefoot on the morass. ♡

Fast forwarding to later in life, I had chosen a career, that meant more time indoors, in an office, and in front of a computer with my cellphone always nearby.

Time in nature dramatically decreased and time spent in electromagnetic radiation multiplied. It didn't take long before the first pneumonia hit me and with it, sinus problems, asthma and IBS (Irritable Bowel Syndrome). To fight the symptoms the doctors prescribed tons of medicine. Some medications made sense, but not all of them did.

In addition to my downward health spiral, I spent a couple of years in Stockholm with electromagnetic smog, harmful particles in the air, and the multitude of germs in the public transportation. That was the last the nail in the coffin, I had had enough.

But there are two sides of every coin. Tough periods during my health journey gave me so much personal experience, knowledge and a desire for change. It motivated me to find knowledge, experiment and share what I had learned.

The struggle and success have given me the power to create a positive change and development for myself and my fellow people in the world.

Part one

Consciously Barefoot

Chapter 1. Earthing /Grounding

"The human is a bioelectronic being"

To Ground yourself

It means that you are in direct contact with the Earth, for example walking Barefoot on grass, sand, soil or rocks. Just like humans have done for eons of time. To swim in the rivers and lakes is another good way to Ground yourself. The Earth underneath us, is an unlimited source of healing energy in the form of free electrons. This is an already established scientific fact, but still something that most of us might not know.

To be Grounded, means you are in direct contact with the Earth and you are absorbing the free electrons. Going back in history, we walked Barefoot or in boots with leather soles, we spent a lot more time outside and bathed in the oceans and lakes. Today we walk with shoes or boots with insulated rubber soles on asphalt, live in houses that have insulated wooden or plastic floors and sleep without contact with the Earth.

Why walk Barefoot, what happens?

The human is a bioelectronic being. Our body conducts electric current, which means that electrons can move through the body. Just like Earth, the body is mostly water and minerals, which are excellent conductors of electrons. Your whole body with its cells and organs works electronically. Like in animals and plants it is electromagnetic pulses and weak currents that run all functions. We measure for example the brain´s electric activity with EEG, and the heart´s electrical activity with EKG. The E in EEG and EKG stands for electric. We could say that our bodies are constructed to be in direct contact with the Earth. When you have recurring contact, the electrons in the body will readjust and stabilize the body's natural electric condition. If the body isn't in contact, its physiological processes might not work as intended, which in its turn can lead to different diseases.

By using heat cameras that register small changes in the body temperature, it is possible to observe the process that takes place in the body, when negatively charged electrons reaches your body via contact with the Earth. Positively charged inflammatory radicals are eliminated and the body can return to its natural balance.

No animals walk with shoes!

In the beginning of time, all mammals walked Barefoot. With time the humans discovered that it might be nice to protect their feet against sharp objects and heat. The indigenous people in different parts of the world, used animal skins that they made their shoes of. Since skin is a leading material they were in contact with the Earth.But in the end of the 19th century, shoes started being manufactured in factories and the soles were made out other materials than leather. When the plastic and chemical industry took over, shoes became what separated us from the healing electrons of the Earth. There are many theories about that it's exactly because we are walking in non-conductive, insulated shoes, that causes us to more and more develop the chronic illnesses that are troubling humans. Isn't it interesting that animals don't have any of the chronic illnesses that we humans have? Could it be related to Earth contact?

Clint Ober

The discovery of the important health benefits with Earthing took place in 1998 by Clint Ober, a retired cable TV businessman. After fighting a deadly disease in 1993, that nearly cost him his life, he spent most of his coming years to find answers and stimulate research related to Earthing/Grounding and the health benefits of electrons. Ober seems to be the first one to consciously focus on research to confirm the connection in modern, scientific terms. He collaborated with researchers and experts within electrophysiology, cellular biology and biophysics. Throughout the years, a number of scientific studies have been presented that show unique and fascinating results on how electrons contribute to health within physiology, sleep, blood chemistry, and that electrons can heal inflammation. In the book *Earthing: The Most Important Health Discovery Ever* the writers Clinton Ober, Stephen T. Sinatra and Martin Zucker describe the benefits that being in contact with the Earth's healing power and energy can bring.

What does conduct material mean?

I mentioned above that shoes are no longer conductive when they are made from rubber or other chemicals. Conductivity is the ability in a matter, to load or conduct electric current. Matters that can conduct current are called conductors.

All metals conduct current, silver and copper the best. Also, water, rocks and the human body conduct current. Matters that don't conduct current are called insulators. Examples of those are rubber, porcelain, plastic, air, wood and asphalt. So, in order to be Grounded, you either need to be Barefoot directly on the ground, or only have a material between the foot and the Earth that is of leading material. Of course, you can use whichever body part you want, but researchers have seen that it is particularly the foot that is created to be like an antenna for the healing electrons. The sole of the foot has thousands of sensory points that with their sensitivity receives the electrons and then transmits them to all bodily organs and functions.

What is EMF?

Electromagnetic fields (EMF) is a concept you use when you talk about electric voltage and magnetic radiation. It is sometimes also just called electromagnetic radiation. If there is a difference in the voltage between one or two points, we have an electric field. As soon as electricity goes through some kind of conductor, there is also a magnetic field. Electromagnetic field is the generic name for these. This is a very simplified explanation.

Our modern surroundings are full of electromagnetic radiation, from computers, cell phones, cell towers, telephone masts, radio and TV broadcasts, wireless networks, Bluetooth, power lines, electric installations and other electronic devices. This electromagnetic radiation creates an electric tension in our bodies, which can disturb the billions of electric signals that are a vital part of bodily function. By connecting us to the Earth we can dramatically reduce this tension, since we are then protected by the enormous electric charge of the Earth.

What can be damaging with EMF?

More and more people feel unhealthy in an IT environment and when they use electronic devices. Common symptoms are skin problems, headache, flu like symptoms, nausea, vertigo or light sensitivity. Many people get symptoms stamming from the nervous system; perceived stress, impaired short-term memory, problems concentrating and abnormal tiredness/exhaustion.

All electronic devices transmit electromagnetic fields. Cell phones and equipment for wireless communication transmit high frequency electromagnetic radiation and microwaves. A lot of research results show that electromagnetic fields and microwave radiation can seriously affect our health.

A growing number of researchers, experts and doctors share the view that radiation is linked to many health risks like cancer and brain damage. The group of experts and researchers that claim it is not dangerous, are in many cases financially tied to the telecom, electricity or military industry. We can compare this with the tobacco and chemical industry. Like them the telecom industry has connected themselves to many loyal researchers to lobby for them. This limited group of experts has gained a big influence and are dominating the majority of expert investigations, in Sweden as well as in the EU and the WHO.

Glossary

Free radicals - positively charged molecules that are missing an electron. Affecting health and aging negatively, give oxidative stress, like rusting from the inside. Chronically increased levels hurt the cells and can lead to inflammatory diseases.

Electron - negatively charged micro particles. They give the surface of the Earth a naturally negative charge. They neutralize the free radicals.

Ions - negatively or positively charged molecules or atoms.

Resistance - resistance to current. The body has low resistance and thus conducts current easily.

Conductivity - the ability in a matter to load or lead electric current.

The bioelectronic nature of the body - we live and function electrically on an electric planet. Just like the Earth, the body is mostly water and minerals that both are excellent conductors of electrons.

AC - Alternating current. An electric current which periodically reverses direction.

DC - Direct current. All electronic demands DC, flows only in one direction.

Electricity - a form of energy, requiring charge, current and resistance.

Electric current - charges moving towards each other.

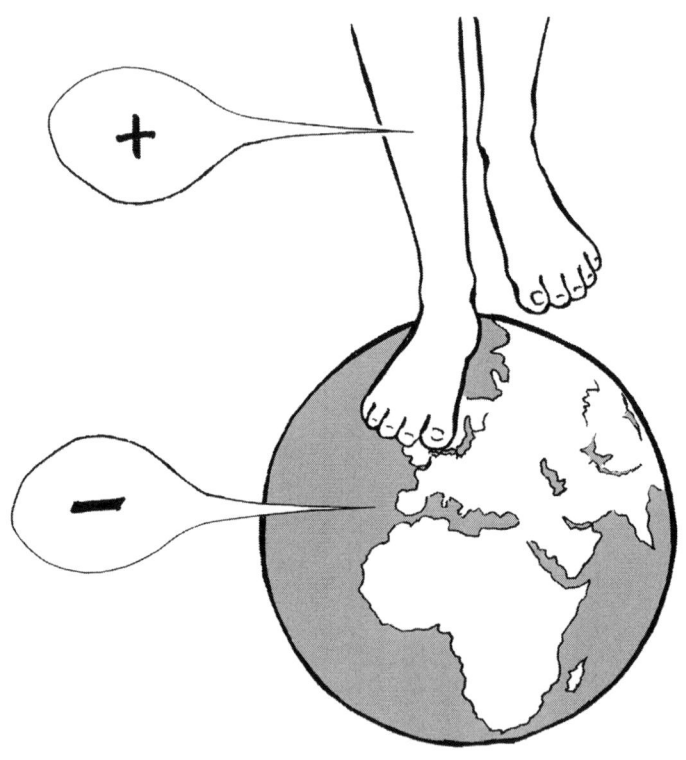

Nature always tries to even out all differences.
The body is filled with positively charged molecules – PLUS.
The Earth, Tellus, is filled with negatively charged electrons – MINUS.

Electric charge - difference in charge between two points, the bigger difference the higher the charge. Measured in voltage.

* * *

Planet Earth's land and ocean areas are filled with an endless supply of free electrons that are constantly renewed, it is the natural electric potential of the Earth.

When our conductive body is in direct contact with the surface of the Earth, our body is charged with the Earth's free electrons. We refill our bodies with electrons, if our body has too few of them. When two conductive objects come in contact with each other, for example my feet and the Earth, electrons will move from where there is a surplus of electrons, to where there are too few and the electric potential is equalized. The body is equalized and maintain the electronic potential of the Earth.

The closer you Ground an area of the body, and fill it up with electrons, the faster is the healing process. If, for example, your knee is inflamed, you can ground the knee so that the electrons need to go less distance. The Earth electrons are filled with extra energy, they have high energy. We can call them supercharged electrons.

The closer you are to the Earth surface, the more electrons you can fill up with. If you open your door on the bottom floor, they come into your room freely. When you open your door on the tenth floor they also enter, but substantially fewer of them.

Ground currents, the subtle currents of the Earth, or the so called global electrical circuitry, includes clouds and the whole atmosphere. This never-ending energy source of free electrons is refilled and reaches the Earth surface through rain and thousands of lightning strikes, continually all over the planet. This electric charge, rises and falls with the solar position. This means that it is more positive and filled with energy during the day, and less at night, which is beneficial for sleeping. The daily pattern of high and low electric charge is directing the inner bodily mechanisms that adjust cycles of sleep and alertness, and the production of hormones and maintenance of health.

Chapter 2. Why should we Ground ourselves?

"A complicated problem doesn't need a complicated solution"

René Manuel Medina, Kinesiologist

Health effects

Research has the last years looked for and found different interesting proof that we, as humans can benefit a lot from the Earth's electrons. The biggest reason why I have become so interested in the effects of Earthing or Grounding that is also called, is that I experience fast and positive results! During the years I have experimented with different methods and diets, to reduce the suffering of chronic inflammation. Amongst others I have tried, are Western and Eastern medicine, as well as Ayurvedic Medicine. I have an education in kinesiology, healing, jin shin jyutsu, hair mineral analysis and yoga. All these nice pieces of the puzzle give their different answers. But what I see give the absolutely best effect is to spend as much time as possible outside, and when I'm Barefoot it gives the significantly fastest results. I also become calmer, feel more stable mentally, breathe deeper, feel more awake and sleep better at night, which in its turn strengthens the immune system and the healing power of the body.

Nowadays there are numerous research studies that show that an addition of electrons can relieve chronic inflammation, reduce pain and help with sleeping. There are studies where heat cameras have been used to follow the white and red blood cells activity before and during Earthing. After only 20 minutes, it can be observed that they instead of being stuck in groups, they start to move and be active. White blood cells have great impact on healing inflammation.

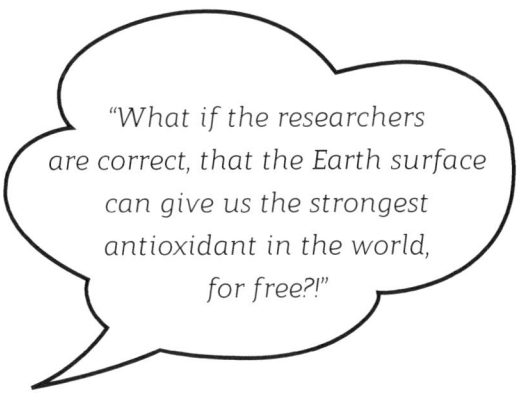

"What if the researchers are correct, that the Earth surface can give us the strongest antioxidant in the world, for free?!"

Antioxidants

Antioxidants is the generic term for substances that have the ability to catch and incapacitate the free oxygen radicals that are formed in the body. The radicals are good in balanced amounts, but today many of us are filled with too many radicals, from for example EMF, and this is not good. We get the antioxidants through food and they are characterized by giving food, strong colors. Lingonberry and blueberry are two examples of food that contain a lot of antioxidants, while cucumber has few. You find antioxidants primarily in berries, fruit and vegetables. By walking Barefoot or in other ways absorb the Earth electrons, we get the same healing effect that the antioxidants give us, a treasure that researchers now are finding proof for.

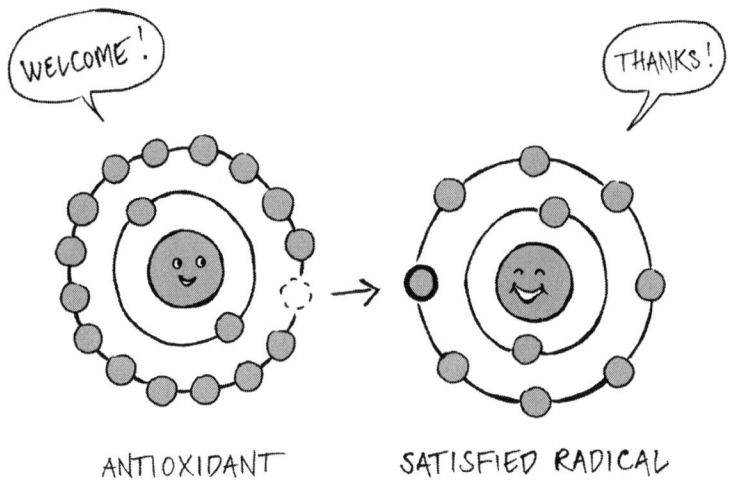

ANTIOXIDANT   SATISFIED RADICAL

The best way to Ground yourself in order to get access to the most possible antioxidants is if you swim in the ocean! The salty water is filled with the healing electrons, antioxidants. Or if you walk Barefoot in the water so the salty water flows over your feet, while you sink into the wet sand. Lakes also have high levels of antioxidants even if the levels are lower than in saltwater oceans. As soon as you spend time outside in contact with the Earth you get electrons into your body. The electrons give the Earth a natural charge. They neutralize the free radicals. We could say that the electrons of the Earth can be "the world's strongest antioxidant".

Chronic inflammation and electron deficiency

There are two different types of inflammation, acute and chronic. The acute inflammation is caused by a reaction of the body to injurious stimuli. It means that plasma and white blood cells, get to the damaged tissue, causing swelling, redness, heat and pain. This is good and means that the body is gathering power to heal the acute inflammation. The chronic inflammation is not good. We can explain it like this:

Your immune system protects you against disease, bacteria and virus. White blood cells and other specialized cells help destroy invading microorganisms and injured tissue. The free radicals, or sometimes called only called radicals, take part in the rescue mission. When we have the correct levels of radicals, they are important and significant for our bodies, but if they are to many then they become harmful. Radicals are molecules that are hunting for electrons. Radicals need one or more electrons to stabilize their molecular structure. Normally the radicals' molecules receive their electrons by peeling them off from disease induced organisms and damaged tissue. This means that when the molecule is hunting electrons, it kills harmful bacteria that we want to get out of our bodies and the molecules breaks down damaged cells so they can be removed.

Radicals play an important part in the immune defense, but it can become problematic when the process fails to slow down the activity after the job is done. They can continue to attack and oxidize healthy tissue. The immune system puts in an extra gear and send more white blood cells which produce even more free radicals. This is the vicious circle that researchers now think points to that inflammation, chronic diseases and the aging process is caused by too much activity from the radicals. Could it be that we humans suffer from an electron deficiency? That there not enough free electrons at hand to satisfy the radicals? This can cause a reaction that is manifested as chronic inflammation. The immune system attacks its owner - you. A destructive process takes place and continues to silently develop and leads to auto immune diseases that are difficult to treat.

Today there are numerous diseases and symptoms that are related to chronic inflammation, to name a few we have: allergies, Alzheimer, ALS (Lou Gehrig's disease), anemia, arthritis, asthma, autism, pancreatic inflammation, cancer, type 1 and type 2 diabetes, fibromyalgia, cardiovascular disease, multiple sclerosis, renal failure, psoriasis, pain. Common bowel diseases, such as Crohn's disease and IBS.

Since we started wearing shoes, there is an increase in these diseases. Is there a correlation?

Medicine against aging

The fact that we can counteract inflammation thanks to Earthing enables us to live a longer and more comprehensive life. Theories that the oxidative damage caused by radicals speeds up aging can be found in studies done already during the fifties. There they look at aging as a result of the accumulated damage on the body caused by radicals. As I mentioned earlier, the radicals are missing an electron, which is what they get from the ground. With the help of negative electrons, the free radicals are transformed to powerful antioxidants.

Pets and Earthing

It is of outmost importance that all animals get to absorb the healing electrons of the Earth! If you have an indoor cat, I recommend that you let it out every day, so it gets in contact with the Earth. We, who have many years of experience from different animals, can confirm, that there is a deep fundamental instinct in the animals to get help from the healing power of the Earth when they get sick. Countless times during my life, we have found our lambs or sheep that have dug a hole in the moist soil and laid down in it to regain strength. The same goes for dogs, they dig a healing hole in the ground, where they lie down and receive the powerful electrons.

Pregnant women, children and Earthing

Today different wireless devices have taken over our homes, schools and workplaces. The questions surrounding all this radiation are many. We cannot be certain that this radiation is harmless, that wireless technique is risk free. To this you can add numerous studies and reports, expert opinions and compilations that say that there are "strong suspicion of injuries". The radiation we are assumed to tolerate is million billion (1 000 000 000 000 000) times (or more!) stronger than the natural background radiation, and the results that have been published in the biomedical literature is, in many cases, particularly scary. Environment and health agencies from all over the world agree, that children and fetuses, are especially sensitive to different environmental factors. There are critical phases during their development when microwave radiation permanently can damage for example the development of the brain. The nervous system continues to develop all through the teens. The heads of children absorb more radiation and their cell conversion rate is higher. Children and teens that use a cell phone run a higher risk than adults. Children are especially sensitive; a child's head can absorb 2-3 times more radiation than the head of a grown man. Don't use wireless babysitter device, since they also transmit microwave radiation. Don't use cell phones or wirelessly connected computers when you breastfeed or holding a baby in your arms.

*"Show compassion!
Don't use the cell phone
or a wirelessly connected computer
in the vicinity of pregnant women,
infants or small children!"*

It is obvious that bees and ants understand this as they runaway when exposed to radiation! It is time for us to do the same! Children are the most important asset every generation has! Further ahead in the book you will get advice on how we can reduce and protect ourselves from EMF and other radiation indoors.

Reduce pain

When the natural processes in the body are balanced through Earthing this can have many positive effects. I have taken part in many case histories, research studies and theories on Earthing. My curiosity has motivated me to try different Earthing methods when I have been ill or felt pain. When I suffered an ear infection, I put conductive plates of the type TENS electrodes on the ear and cheek, connected them with a Grounding cable to the water radiator, hence causing electrons to go to the inflamed area where they could contribute to reduce the pain and stop the inflammation. It still hurt, but it only took a short while to get pain free and my eardrum didn't rupture, nor did I need antibiotics. Menstrual cramps can be very painful. Also, here I have noticed a significant improvement with Earthing, with the positive side effect of not needing to use pain medicine.

Other examples where I have experienced Earthing to reduce pain and quicken healing is in the case of sprained ankles, neck problems, gout and headache. To lie down on the ground, or dig your feet deep into the sand, creates a feeling of calm and harmony for both body and soul and can reduce pain.

Chapter 3. How to Ground yourself

> *"Find your way to have skin contact with the Earth."*

Just go outside

The best way to Ground yourself is to go outside and let the skin have contact with the Earth. The easiest way is to walk Barefoot outside on grass, soil, sand or rocks. The moister the grass or soil is, the better your contact with it will be. Many of us are used to walking Barefoot, enjoying the pleasure of it, and knowing that the body answers quickly to the contact with Mother Earth. If you are one of them that never tried this, you have a lot to look forward to. Start slowly by walking Barefoot on sand or on grass. The sole of the foot is very sensitive, but it is good for the skin to walk Barefoot. Be careful if the sand is too hot, so you don't burn the skin.

On asphalt it can be a good idea to wear shoes. Asphalt is a petrochemical product that cannot transport electrons and it contains substances that might be harmful to our bodies.

A good rule is: Everything you choose for your skin to be in contact with, you should be able to eat. Everything you put on your skin, including makeup, sunscreen and shaving gel should be edible in order to not disturb the cells or the bodily functions and organs.

Our magical feet

In our modern time we can feel unaccustomed to taking off our shoes and walk Barefoot. But before the shoes and tall buildings came, the natural thing was to walk Barefoot or with shoes made of skin and to sleep on the ground.

The sole of our foot is so cleverly constructed. It is remarkably sensitive and is created to receive electrons, touch, heat and cold in order to transport it out through the bodily organs, cells and functions. It is said that the sole of the foot contains more than 200 nerve endings per square centimeter. The same is true for animals. Our feet and the animal paws are made to be receptors for the free electrons of the Earth that float into our bodies, balances and creates health.

Walking and running Barefoot

As I wrote in the introduction I have been fascinated by Barefoot runners for a long time. It takes courage and a strong will to run without shoes, on trails with pine needles, pebbles and rocks, mud and different vegetation. I think it is easier than we think.

Something happens to us humans, when we take off our shoes, when we stand Barefoot on the ground and become a part of the Earth's bioelectric energy field. Besides all the health benefits something within us softens. Our body, mind and senses open up and become part of the nature around us. With shoes we can move with fast, hard, unconscious steps anywhere we want. We don't have to care about what ends up underneath our foot, what the impression on the grund will be. In a way that mirrors how we are moving forward on the planet right now. When we have bare feet, we need to be curious about what is in front of and underneath it. The whole sole of the foot awakens and starts to collaborate to find the softest trails and creates calm, security and stability.

The impression of the feet that we make, can barely be seen, because we land mostly on the front foot, easy like a soft touch, of the ground. We focus our eyesight close and far, in order to make strategies and plan for what comes further ahead. Our other senses follow the smooth wave and opens up for smells, sounds and tastes. The breathing gets deeper and the relaxing system celebrates together with the destressing hormones.

My advice is to start slowly. If you haven't walked without shoes, or used the many small muscles, ligaments and tendons of the foot, you can overdo it and damage yourself. To walk, jog or run without shoes, strengthens the muscles in the metatarsus. To mix some Barefoot runs with normal runs, is common among elites and regular exercise makes the feet stronger. We get stimulation through Barefoot walking that sends electrons to the body and gives a natural massage that can be compared to reflexology, creating harmony and balance in both body and soul, and it increases our well-being on every level. For a while I lived close to a sports field. I really enjoyed running Barefoot, round and round, in big circles on the big grass field. It is so enjoyable for the foot to get to feel the soft grass, moist, cold and warmth. To get the most electrons you should look for moist grass.

Ocean and lakes give an electron bath

The most efficient Earthing is when you swim in oceans, lakes and rivers!

The biggest effect is when you swim in saltwater. This is because salt water contains ions that conduct current. The concentration of ions determines the conductivity. The more salt and minerals, the more ions and higher conductivity. The ions end up in the ocean like this:

The sun lifts clean water from the salty sea and from the ground up to the clouds in the sky. The clean water then reaches the land again as rain and rinse salts and minerals from mountains, forest and soil. Streams and rivers are refilled with this water that is rich in minerals, they create lakes and finally reaches the ocean again which is the end station. During this long journey from mountain to ocean the concentration of salt and minerals have increased. With that also the amount of electrically charged ions that make the water more conductive. The ocean consists of 96 % water and 4 % salt.

If you have the opportunity to swim in either the ocean or sweet water lakes, it gives a nice sensation and you should try to stay as long as you can.

This is where I feel that my inclination to hesitate to get into the water is helping me. I'm one of those people that spend a long time by the shoreline, trying to get used to the temperature. Then I walk further and further out, before I finally decide to jump in. This means that for a long time I'm taking in electrons via feet and legs. Far longer than if I were to run out, immerse myself in the water and run up again on the beach. But I'm practicing being braver. I want to be able to jump in and lay in the sea of electrons, swim for a long time and enjoy it.

There are two more ways to refill on electrons:

1. Stay in the warm sand close to the shoreline, dig your feet as deep down as you can in the sand so you get to the moist sand.

2. Sit or lie on the beach close the shoreline with your feet in the water.

The thinner your towel or fabric consisits of that you have between you and the Earth, the more electrons will come to you.

Skin contact is always preferable.

Earthing indoors

The simplest way for home owners to get Grounded, is to move the sunchair from the wooden deck to the lawn. While you drink your morning coffee you can allow your toes to dig down into the dewy grass. The longer you stay there, the more the electrons will fill up your body, or take off your shoes and socks while you work in the garden. It is lovely to feel the soil under the soles of your feet. Also, remove your gloves when you are weeding or working with the soil so that your hands are in contact with the electrons. Some dirt under the nails is also good for boosting your supply of protective bacteria for your intestinal flora. During colder days a greenhouse can be the best escape. Often, they are built directly on the ground or on a stone floor without a plastic moisture barrier in the foundation. There you will be Grounded if you remove your shoes and socks.

For you who live in an apartment there are other ways to Ground yourself, while you drink your morning coffee. Bring your sunchair from the balcony down to the garden and enjoy your coffee Barefoot. What if all your neighbors also did this, what a wonderful social start of the day!

Or hold on to the sink. It is actually a fact, that the faucet and sink Ground you. Maybe this sounds weird, but it works since the water and the copper pipes leading the water to you, start in the foundation of the house in contact with the soil. This means that if you put your hand by the faucet or on the sink you will be Grounded. The same thing goes for water heated radiators. Also, those are connected with the Earth, through conductive pipes, leading the water to your radiator.

Oftentimes radiators are painted. The paint hinders the electrons from moving, which hinders their ability to Ground you. However, oftentimes you find parts of the pipes without paint close to the radiator thermostat, where you can Ground yourself. If your radiators are built during recent years, you might be unlucky to find that the water is lead to the radiator via plastic pipes. Then you cannot Ground yourself via your radiator.

You can create Earthing indoors by bringing it in through the window from the Earth with a ground rod and cable. I will explain more in the chapter "Earthing in colder climates".

In the forest

A walk in the forest will do so much more for your health and experience, if you take off your shoes. If your feet are not used to the different surfaces it can be wise to start carefully. Find trails that are comfortable. Pine needles, soil, sand, grass, flat rocks and moss are usually a good start. Start the habit of spending part of your walk or run Barefoot, and increase the Barefoot part walk by walk.

To walk or jog by the shoreline Barefoot is great. You are then in contact with the Earth that is moist or even wet, which significantly helps to Ground you.

A common question is, if Earthing works when you hug a tree? The answer is both yes and no. Wood is not conductive, hence not leading electrons. If you on the other hand get in contact with the sap of the tree by touching a branch or a leaf you will be Earthed. This works, since the sap is in contact with the Earth, through the roots of the tree. To hug a tree gives us so much contact with nature and ourselves, so absolutely, hug trees as much as you can!

Beloved thunder

Another powerful source of Earthing is thunder! This is a phenomenon that many of us have the experience of being affected by. At my home in Västerbotten, in Northern part of Sweden, people knew exactly when a thunderstorm was approaching. Headache, tiredness and a feeling of frustration were some of the symptoms. It has a natural explanation in that the atmosphere has a high positive charge before the thunder takes off. The charge is the same that we get charged with since our bodies like the Earth mostly consist of water and minerals. Human beings are very conductive, and it is easy for electrons to rush through and fill us. As soon as the relieving rain arrives after the lightning, we are practically showered with negative electrons and we feel so much better in body and spirit. Considering there are around 5 000 lightning strikes per minute around the world, one can understand how the Earth again and again, is recharged with the healing negative electrons. So, taking a walk in the rain after a thunderstorm is a real source of power. Miraculously healthy and completely free!

Chapter 4. Reduce and avoid EMF at home and at work

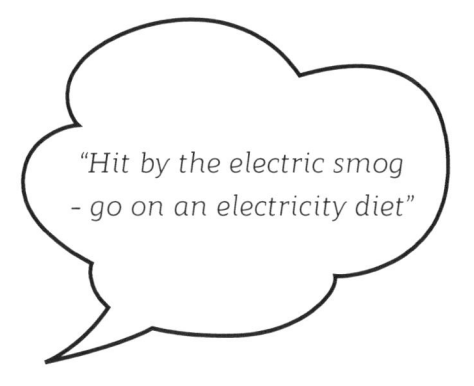

"Hit by the electric smog - go on an electricity diet"

Are we being naive and blind?

We should all be conscious that we are being exposed to EMF from electric devices mostly everywhere today. Indoors as well as outdoors. In our homes, at work, at the cinema, in the store, at the gym, in the car, etc. Besides EMF we also have radiation from Wi-Fi, cellphones, computers, 3-4-5 G network. As

I said earlier, this is a big topic and research has made some progress.

Electric smog is becoming a more well-known expression that describes what we are exposed to, perhaps without being too conscious about how or even that it affects us, our bodies and health. I wonder, could electric smog be compared to the cigarette smoke we were exposed to as small children? During the fifties, sixties and seventies, few had the slightest idea that second hand smoke could be harmful, whether in the car, at home or at the restaurant. The carcinogenic cigarette smoke would later end many lives prematurely. Could there be a similar naive relationship to EMF and other radiation today? I am very worried this is the case. But I am happy there are many ways to reduce our exposure. As soon as we are conscious, we can act and reduce our daily exposure. When we add "getting connected to" the Earth surface with natural Earthing, we can achieve a completely new sense of well-being and health.

How can we measure EMF?

So, how can I with such certainty know that we are affected by EMF? Can we even say that we are affected? Or should we say we are part of it? The last sentence might be a better representation, since we are conductive and become part of the EMF field, we are in.

I really want to recommend that you read more at the website Powerwatch.com. It is a forum for a small group of knowledgeable engineers, scientists and medical researchers who are concerned about the consequences of irradiated 'blue world' we are creating. They have been researching the links between electromagnetic fields (EMFs) and health risks for about 30 years and are completely independent of government and industry. Many that have had access to meters of electric charge, a voltmeter or multimeter, have seen this, but Erich W. Fischer in Germany gave the method a name: the Fischer method. He started using it in the beginning of 1980 to help creating a better electric environment.

There are many movie clips on the internet that show how to measure the charge, we are a part of, when we have electric devices in our vicinity. Many of them are recorded by Clint Ober, author of the book "Earthing". I spent many evenings by the computer watching the movies on the internet, and I became very curious. I wanted to see with my own eyes, I wanted to test and see all the possible situations what happens, how my conductive body becomes part of EMF.

It took me quite a long time to find a multimeter, that I could feel with certainty, measured our charge in the body. Finally, with the help of an electric engineer, I found my multimeter that has become a loyal and dear friend. With time, thanks to the meter, I have learnt to estimate, even without meter, what levels of volt surrounds and hence also are in us. I must say it was a shock to discover the levels of current our bodies become part of when we are in environments with electric devices, especially ungrounded ones. The worst shock was when I measured our apartment, since here we have grounded outlets only in kitchen and bathroom. Ungrounded outlets are horrible, I promise you. So, in our bedroom, living room and hallway it is not possible to Ground our electronic devices.

According to the Swedish "Elsäkerhetsverket" (it is a government authority for electrical safety) there are regulations that demand the usage of grounded outlets when building a new house, renovating and expansions of electric buildings, but this was put in place only the 1st of July 1994 in Sweden.

This means that all schools, apartment houses, and houses built before 1994, can have ungrounded outlets in all rooms except kitchen and bathroom, i.e. wet spaces. I have gotten more and more requests to visit peoples' home to help them assess their EMF levels. When we see how and where it comes from it is usually simple that with small measures we can reduce and completely remove EMF, from different rooms and spaces in the house.

Here you can see a table of the measurements I have taken in our apartment:

Measurements number of volts in the body		
Kitchen table	Hand on the table	Hand on the computer
Without computer	0,061	
WIth computer	0,269	16.53
With computer, charged in grounded outlet	0,093	0,055
With computer, charged in ungrounded outlet	1,046	50,93
Kitchen		
Close to stove, refrigerator, dish washer	0,123	
Holding the sink	0,018	
Living room sofa		
Computer		
Without computer, no lamp	0,062	
Without computer + a floor lamp	0,357	
With computer + a floor lamp	0,371	
With grounded cord	0,223	0,071
With ungrounded cord	50,31	87,03

Cell phone		
Without cell phone only floor lamp	0,558	
Cell phone + charger in ungrounded outlet	0,946	29,15
Bedroom		
With only outlet near the floor	0,064	
With ungrounded string lights	0,026	
With bed lamp ungrounded	0,064	

What we can see and learn from my measurements is that as long as you are among grounded devices there are lower levels of EMF. In the kitchen you have both dishwasher, stove, fridge and freezer. They all have a cord that is grounded and connected to a grounded outlet. This means they have low levels of EMF. Also, in the bathroom with washing machine and dryer, they are connected to grounded outlets. When I sit by the kitchen table, I am close to the kitchen lamp and it is not grounded so my body has a charge, however it is low.

It is also interesting to see what happens when I have my computer in front of me charging, with or without cord in different outlets in the wall, grounded or ungrounded. It is important to know that the cord to my computer is grounded (see image of grounded/ungrounded cords further ahead in the book). When I put the cord in the grounded outlet, we can see that also I become in some sense Grounded, the charge decreases also in relation to the kitchen lamp. The cord is long and stretches into the living room. I now put it in the ungrounded outlet. What happens? The obviously unpleasant shows in the meter. I become aware of how strong the field of charge I am exposed to is. **The conclusion is that we should always have grounded outlets in the walls and grounded cords to our electronic devices.**

In the bedroom we measured the level of radiation by measuring through the walls, to make sure there are no built-in electric cords in the walls against the next apartment, which we were lucky enough to find there was not. That can be a nasty source of EMF radiation that you are exposed to for 7-10 hours a day, i.e. the time you spend in bed.

We moved our bed lamps, so they are further away from the bed, and the cord is not plugged in when we fall asleep. Choosing the right bulb is also important.

Last, but not least, NO cellphones in the bedroom during the night!

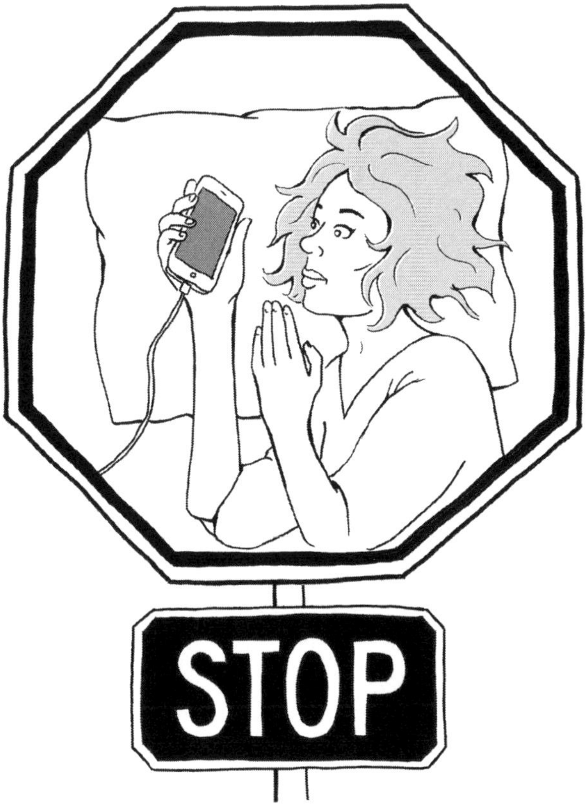
STOP

Advice for a healthier indoor environment

1. Never charge your cell phone when you are holding it, the charging cord is not grounded.

2. Put the cell phone on flight mode as often as possible.

3. Disconnect Bluetooth and Wi-Fi on your cell phone and computer.

4. Make sure your computer has a grounded cord for charging, and that the cord is connected to a grounded outlet.

5. Unplug all cords to your electronic devices, that are not grounded when you are not using them.

6. If you are not sure if your bedroom has hidden cables in the walls, ask for help to measure this.

7. If you have a specific fuse for your bedroom, shut it off during the night to not get electricity to that room.

8. Reduce the number of cords and electronic devices.

9. Change your ungrounded outlets to grounded ones if you can.

10. Shut off all equipment by unplugging them, there is EMF in the cord all the way to the power button.

11. Remove unnecessary electronic equipment from your bedroom, like alarm clocks, lamps, phones, computers and TVs.

12. Put your stationary router and Wi-Fi on a timer so it shuts off during the night.

13. Use a cord from your router during the day.

14. Don't let children be close to an iPad or a smartphone.

15. Try to have skin contact with the Earth and walk Barefoot as often as you can.

How do I know what are grounded outlets and cords?

To know how it looks in your country, you can find information and clear pictures of it in Wikipedia, the free encyclopedia, "Mains electricity by country" includes a list of countries and territories, with the plugs, voltages and frequencies they commonly use for providing electrical power to appliances, equipment, and lighting typically found in homes and offices".

These pictures and descriptive text show examples from Sweden.

To the left is an image of a **grounded outlet**. As you can see there are two small metal hooks on the round plastic wall in the outlet. That is the feature of a grounded outlet. The metal hooks are connected to a cord on the back of the outlet that is grounding. We buy electricity from our supplier, that feels like a no-brainer. What we seldom know is that we also buy the grounding from them. To have good protective grounding is the basis to increase the electrical safety in the household. Without grounding, electronic equipment and installations can be damaged and peoples' lives put at risk.

Grounding makes sure that leakage current securely are led to ground and automatized solutions like earth fault switches can shut down an electrical system if an error occurs. It is especially important to make sure the grounding is working properly during thunderstorms and in the case of high levels of faulty currents, to protect both humans and equipment.

Here is an **ungrounded outlet**. You can see there are no metal hooks on the round walls on the inside of the outlet. Hence there is nothing leading the current to ground. The outlet in the wall with the two holes is usually called "female electrical outlet".

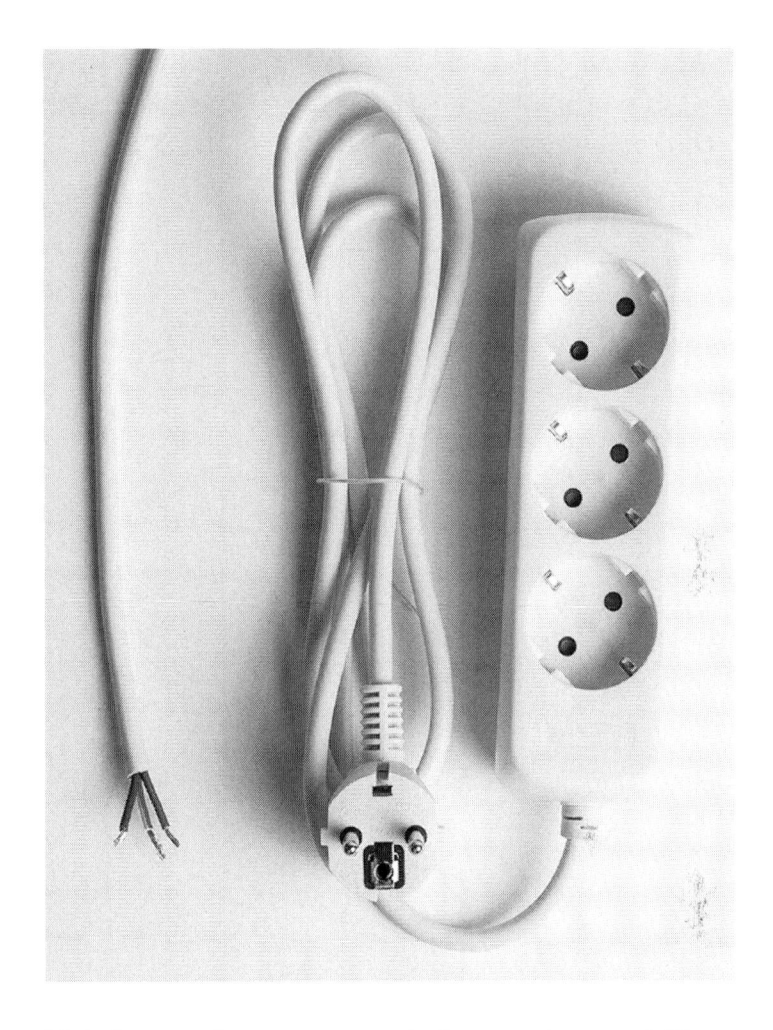

This image shows a grounded extension cord. Here you can see what a **grounded strap** can look like. With its two spikes it can be called "male". On the strap there are small, shiny parts of metal on the side of the round plastic surface. When we put the cord in the outlet the metal of the cord touches the grounding of the outlet, and this makes your equipment grounded. The cord feels a bit thicker since underneath the plastic surface there are three cables of which one is yellow/green, the one that goes to the grounding.

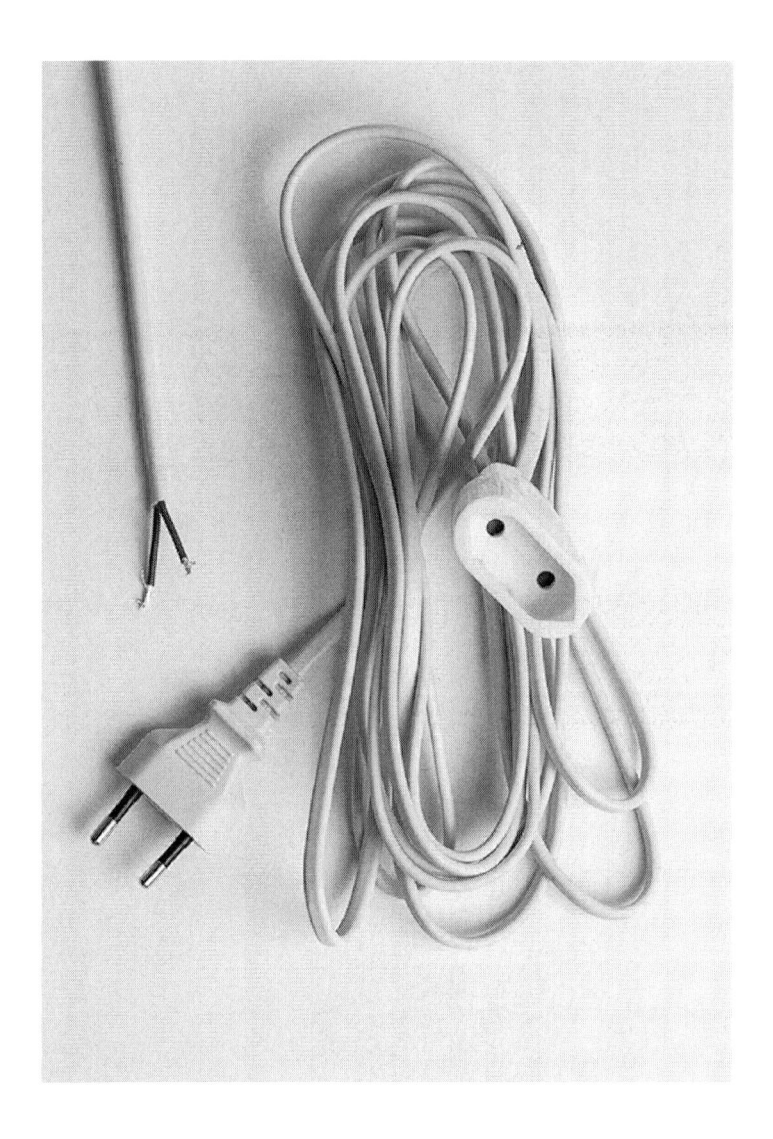

The image to the left shows an ungrounded extension cord. Here you can see how an **ungrounded strap** can look like, it can be round or flat. Often you find these on cords to lamps, cell phone chargers, radios, speakers, printers, kitchen devices like food mixers, processors and electric mixers.

These types of straps don't have any metal parts to connect with the grounding of the outlet. You can also notice that the cord looks flat and thin, this is because it only contains two cables.

Your equipment will not be grounded, if you put a grounded strap in an ungrounded outlet.

Chapter 5. Electrons in cold climates

> "A nail in the ground with a cord to the bed, that's it!

To be Grounded indoors

There are simple solutions to reach healing electrons even if you are indoors. One way is to get them through the window. You can put a leading material like an iron rod or a tall nail in the ground outside your house, preferably some distance from the wall so you can reach moist soil a bit deeper down. Peel the plastic off on a part of the leading cable, attach it to the rod so that they are in contact with each other. Bring the cable into the room through a window or door. If you have water radiators in your house or apartment, you can attach the cable to the unpainted parts of the pipes of the radiator, instead of bringing the cable down to the ground. The water radiator Grounds, because the copper pipes and water lead to soil in your house or apartment.

When you have ensured that you found Grounding in the soil or from the radiator you peel the plastic cover from the other end of the cable that now is indoors. When you now hold the shiny part of the cable with your hand the electrons from the Earth will climb into your body. If it feels weird to hold it with your hand, twist it around your big toe when you sleep at night, or connect it to, whatever conductive material and attach that to your body. You can get a small metal net that you put underneath your sheet, and attach the cable to the net so you can enjoy the electrons the whole night while you sleep.

When you are working by the computer or sitting on the couch reading, you can put your foot on the cable. You can attach a shiny metal object, for example a table knife, so you get a larger area for the electrons to walk over by.

Isn't it amazing that it can be this easy and almost completely for free?

Health with machines and technical equipment

I advocate the simple and down to Earth ways, what all people in the world can afford and what is good for Mother Earth.

Still, I would like to mention what is happening in the technical side of the health world. If you have the finances, there are many things you can buy online, everything from Earthing sheets to QRS mattresses.

The last years we have seen many advanced machines that can help you be more balanced and help the body to heal itself. Dr. Sanna Ehdin explains energy medicine this way:

> *"Just like light we consist of both matter and waves. That is why we can reach our physical part, the body, by affecting the energy part. You can do this with the help from subtle energies, as with healing and qigong, and also via electromagnetic energy in the form of sound and light waves. These energy treatments have the generic term frequency medicine since they operate at different frequencies"*

All living things have a certain frequency and intensity, which means they vibrate at a certain wavelength. You can measure this with an instrument – oscilloscope. The frequency, or tone, is different for different cells, organs and parts of your body. I had the opportunity to borrow a QRS mat (Quantron Resonance System). Simplified, you can say that it is a battery charger for our cells. I was excited to tune in the different frequencies to strengthen different organs and bodily functions. The mat was made by *Novato Medic AB* and they describe the functionality like this:

> "Pulsating electromagnetic therapy, commonly known as PEMF, is energy medicine. Electromagnetic therapy is created according to the Earth's own electromagnetic pulse to improve circulation and cellular turnover. Human bodies are living due to electromagnetic exchange between cells. Brainwaves are measured with EEG tests and heart waves with EKG test. When a person suffers a cardiac arrest, we use a defibrillator to send a therapeutic dose of energy to the heart to restart it. PEMF therapy creates a low frequency pulsating electromagnetic field (PEMF) that charges the cells of the body, enables them to float freely, which then increases their efficiently working surface and improves circulation, acidification and hydration. At the same time the cell's ability to absorb nutrients and remove toxins from the body is improved."

My own beloved machine

Ok, I admit, I bought a machine!

During my time in Stockholm I struggled with the bad quality of air in big cities. I got advice from a friend that suffers from severe asthma, to get an air purifier. He ensured me it worked wonders on indoor air quality. And since I was completely hooked on the magic influence of electrons, the decision was easy. I bought an air purifier that generates billions of electrons per second which are turned into negative ions. The negative ions charge particles in the air like virus, bacteria, pollution, pollen, allergens, etc. negatively. When the particles have become negatively charged, they are attracted by the positively charged collector that works like a giant magnet for particles.

It is an amazing enjoyment to see what gets stuck on the pipe. I get delighted when I rinse off all the nasty particles and know that they are not in my respiratory tract.

Chapter 6. Other aspects of the term Earthing

> "... only the Barefoot will feel the wisdom of the People of the Morass."

To Ground yourself can have many different meanings. To be Grounded and in contact with electrons is an unknown term for most people. I asked my friend Sara Oja, *Nordcirkus*, artist and storyteller: **What do you think about when you hear the word Earthing?**

"To Ground myself". I haven't used that expression before, but since I have gotten the opportunity from you to write about it, I have

started thinking about it. And the more I think about it the more I realize how important the Earth actually is to me. Ashes to ashes, dust to dust. Only that. Without the Earth, neither humans as a species or me as a person would exist. In more than one way the Earth is the basis of my existence. The Earth feeds me and makes me grow. The Earth is the reason I can and want to move, and it has enabled me to think. All that I love I have the Earth to thank for, for example trees and other people. Despite all this I give the Earth very little attention. It has actually very little space in my life. I feel ashamed when I think about it.

There is a saying "To stand firmly with both feet on the ground" that I think about sometimes. I have that as a goal and to me it means something along the lines of being calm, safe and reliable. Unfortunately, this is mostly empty words since I rarely allow myself to just stand calmly and quietly here on the Earth. One reason is that my life has gotten so grown-up and important during the last years. I have filled it with children, a husband, work, friends, family, commitments, expectations and desires.

And for some unconscious reason I therefore don't allow myself to get anchored in the ground. In the grass. On rocks or in mud.

Although that is all I need and want, stand calmly and safely with mud between my toes. But no, most of the time I let myself get pulled away, controlled by the watch, in an insane velocity forward. Or backwards. Or both directions at the same time, and all directions, here and there, between different desires, expectations and demands. This even though it pulls me as far away from the Earth and from myself as possible.

Unfortunately, this is how I've been taught that life should be. That the most important thing is to be on time, to perform and to be the best. I, as many others, have carefully been imprinted with words like growth, profitability and success. And now we are living in the aftermaths; restlessness, uncertainty, worry, anxiety, guilt, shame, tiredness and not too seldom, a strong desire to just get away and drop everything.

Ashes to ashes, dust to dust. We begin and end up in the Earth. But the Earth is also very much the now. Which is a bit strange to think about, since in one way it is a bit too big, but the Earth is always there. Even if I forget or don't think about it. Even if I continue to live my grown-up life with stress, worry and anxiety the Earth is there. All the time. Often less than a meter away. It is there like a guide if I want it. Like a support or possibility to another kind of life. It is there constantly with its ability to heal. With calm and peace, not only at the end of life, but very much in the middle of it and I can at any moment just stop and dig my feet into the ground. That is very, very concrete. The Earth is there. No guilt, no questions. I am welcome if and when I come. And the payoff is often immediate, we have instant contact. As much with grippy soil as with intangible infinity. There is a contact with the eternal and contact with me. With everything alive but most clearly with what is now.

So, Earthing is contact, with the Earth, the eternal and with me. Yes, it is that simple.

Ps. I've also noticed that after a while in contact things can start to be awaken. Seeds of wonder for example. Happiness, joy, sensitivity, sensibility and inspiration. That is apparently what happens when soil, skin and sky touch. Ds"

Let's move from Sara's nice interpretation of Earthing to more mythical thoughts around Grounding.

In the Northern part of Scandinavia, we are getting help from different beings that contribute to our health and well-being. To name a few, we have the

Little people; the Elves, the real, half meter high, with nice wool clothes and knitted hoods. And the People of the Morass, the ones that populated the Earth long before humans. They are said to possess a powerful wisdom. I especially remember a tale about the People of the Morass that we are reminded about still today.

The People of the Morass gathered by the reindeer pasture to the west of the village. Together they took off, passing dry sand dunes with weathered pine trees where the owl had its nests. The mountain birches lured the People of the Morass to stay and enjoy the just unfolded leaves. They enjoyed the scent and the taste that reminded them of the times before the humans came. They strolled over the foggy sand ridges all the way to West Morass. There they gathered to keep the memory of "The great meeting" alive.

This tale has been kept alive by the People of the Morass since the day they came to the Earth Morass life. It is told time and again to always be alive to the carriers of love. One day, when you yourself will get to the morass, maybe you also get to experience the memory of "The great meeting". But remember: *" ... only the Barefoot will feel the wisdom of the People of the Morass."*

From the mystery of the People of the Morass, my thoughts go to what the term Grounding came to mean, due to my own roots on my mother's side. During the war in Norway there was a severe shortage of food and many suffered. My mother who was born in Mo I Rana in Northern part of Norway, in 1924, had eleven siblings and had to endure a lot. I wished she wouldn't have had to. The illnesses were hard to fight, many died already as young. Her older brother Johan suffered from rickets, and it took him four years before he could walk. He wasn't lucky enough to be soil drawn. Little Tilde and other were luckier. Soil drawing was done with the hope that it would lead to healing and survival, as in this little tale from Helgeland's Coast in the northern Norway:

"Tilde was only a small infant when she suffered from rickets. Her mother brought her to a wise woman and asked for help. In the hope that it would help, she was to be soil drawn. They dug a hole through a pile of soil, put the baby on a sheet and dragged her seven times through the hole in the ground while the wise woman prayed over her. It took a few days until all symptoms were gone and the little girl came to live a long and healthy life."

Part two

Conscious everyday Breathing

Chapter 7. Breathing

"It is as stupid to try to eat meatballs with your nose as it is to try to breathe with your mouth"

Anders Olsson

Conscious everyday Breathing

My interest for breathing stems from having had problems with the airways, for the last fifteen years, and I've constantly been looking for an understanding of how to heal.

I've taken Anders Olsson's *Conscious Breathing Instructor Course* and through this been exposed to a treasure of learnings. If you breathe correctly, you'll live longer!

We all know it is important to breathe, that the breath should be deep and not superficial. Many are also doing different breathing exercises connected with yoga or meditation. That is really good! It puts a focus on the breathing and increases consciousness. What I want to add is consciousness of the everyday Breathing. The Breathing is so much more than what most of us think about. And how we breathe everyday has a large effect on our health and well-being.

We are built so we can endure weeks without food, days without water, but without breathing, we can only survive a couple of minutes.

Did you know that we breathe ca 1 000 breaths every hour! That is about 25 000 breaths per day. It is about 10-20 kg, 20-40 lbs. of air, that pass in and out through our system, which is 10 times more than the amount of food we eat. With those numbers in mind, we can understand how important it is with the everyday breathing that we do 24 hours a day.

By becoming conscious of our breathing and improve the way we breathe, we can oxygenate our body in a more efficient way. Then we take control of our breathing and can directly affect our thoughts and feelings, our inner organs like heart, brain and the different bodily functions of the body like muscular movements, digestion and immune defense.

Cells, Breathing and Earthing

We breathe because the cells and organs of the body consume large amounts of oxygen and produce large amounts of carbon dioxide. Our body contains around 100 000 billion cells that make up our organs like heart, liver, lungs and brain. These cells need oxygen, water, nutrients and energy.

The cells are mini engines that need energy to perform their duties. Simplified we can say that the energy comes from the food we eat, is mixed with the air we breathe, and loaded by electrons that are stored in the cellular batteries, the mitochondria, that run the metabolism. The mitochondria are like microscopic power plants. There can be thousands of them in every cell depending on how much energy that cell needs to produce. Heart and kidney cells contain the most mitochondria.

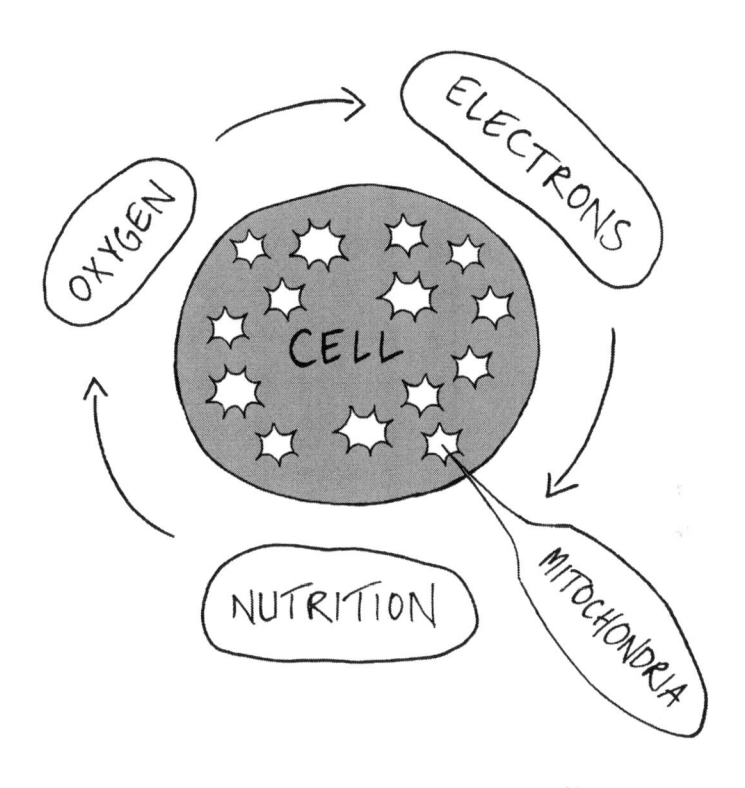

Stephen T Sinatra, M.D., F.A.C.C (*Fellow of American Collage of Cardiology*) is a certified heart specialist focusing on bioenergy. He says in the book *Earthing* that *"I consider that one place where bioelectric energy addition occurs is in the mitochondria."*

Electrons are a part of a complicated process that constantly takes place inside the mitochondria. During this process the electrons collaborate with enzymes and create the substance adenosine triphosphate, ATP, which is the foundational fuel that sustain cells with energy. The cells need this energy to work and repair themselves. When you Ground yourself, you ensure that there are sufficient levels of electrons in the mitochondria. Stephen T Sinatra continues:

> *"Researchers say that these energies filled electrons exist in an excited state. The electrons that are offered by the Earth could be of this type, electrons that are filled to the width with higher energy. The Earth would then supply us not only with more electrons but with super charged electrons!"*

From this we can conclude that the Earth electrons are important to the cells and their power plants, the mitochondria.

The powerful part is that we can multiply the constant work of the mitochondria, by breathing correctly. When we breathe correctly, we get access to greater amounts of oxygen.

I want to recommend the five principles of *Conscious Breathing* by Anders Olsson:

- Through the nose

- With the diaphragm, deep, wide and low

- Slowly

- Rhythmically

- Quietly

I also want to quote Anders Olsson from his book, *Conscious Breathing*, where he writes about how the cells get what they need:

> *"The most efficient way to extract energy from nutrients is with the help of oxygen. The process is called combustion and takes place in the mitochondria of the cell, the energy factory of the body. The majority of our energy need, 90 %, is produced in by combustion of nutrients and oxygen. Mitochondria can be compared to combustion engines. A normal fire can be put out by suffocating it. The reverse is also true, if we add oxygen, we can increase the intensity of a fire. The same principle happens in our body, the more oxygen (and nutrients) that is available for the mitochondria, the more energy is produced.*

Isn't it amazing and logical that the most simple and natural can give the most powerful outcome!

Breathe through your nose and walk Barefoot!

Close your mouth

So HOW should we then breathe our 20-25 000 breaths per day? We could say it with three words: **Close your mouth.** If we want to be clearer, we can add four more: **Breathe through your nose.** I really like the quote by Anders Olsson: *"It is as stupid to try to eat meatballs with your nose, as it is to breathe with your mouth"*.

It is so rewarding to practice Conscious Breathing! I remember I set the target that I would breathe through my nose, deep in the stomach, while waiting for the bus. The first minute always went well, but then, as soon as I started thinking about something else, the breath wasn't where I wanted it. But after a while, maybe a month, I could celebrate that I two times a day for four minutes could breathe consciously. It felt big! With these eight minutes, I got the confidence to dare to expand the moments of breathing through my nose. I practiced on the bus, by the computer, while doing the dishes, etc. It was difficult, with the head full of different thoughts, my breathing couldn't become conscious. It was not until I bought a Relaxator that I fully took the control over my breathing. The Relaxator is a small and handy tool to have in the mouth and breathe through. You can adjust the resistance. With it, I can control my breathing. Besides that, I improve the oxygenation. I prolong the exhalation, which stimulates the vagus nerve and the body's peace and quiet system, which in turn reduce stress and increases the brain capacity to concentrate and focus.

There is only one thing to do! Breathe through the nose!

Why should we breathe through the nose? Because the nose is constructed to be used for exactly breathing. What happens is that the air gets moist and warm, when passing through the nose. The flicker hair takes care of bacteria, viruses and chemicals so they do not get into the lungs. Additionally, the breath is spiced in the sinuses with nitrogen monoxide, which widen the smooth muscle in the trachea, so that the oxygen is more easily transferred to the blood. Breathing through the nose also give a deeper breath, that reaches further down the lungs, so that the full capacity of the lungs is used. There is research today that show that the quality of breathing can affect the recovery of many diseases like asthma, allergy, pain, ache, tiredness, hearth and blood circulation, psychological well-being, sleep apnea, overweight and digestion.

Reduce inflammation

Inflammations that are the cause of many of today's most growing diseases are tightly connected to the quality of your breathing. In the book, *Conscious Breathing* by Anders Olsson we read:

> *"Inflammation is caused by free radicals constantly produced in the body. In case of an inefficient breathing the number of free radical in the cell mitochondria. One reason that the mitochondria are under stimulated by too little oxygen is when the breathing is impaired. Then the leak of free radicals that can damage the cells increases. You can compare the reaction in the body to when metal is affected by rust or when the apple turns brown after being exposed to light and oxygen. During oxidation in the body the inflammation increases in the body, to reduce the damage oxidation causes on the blood vessels. If the oxidation happens faster than the body can cope with, the aging process is accelerated. Free radicals are a necessary part of the immune system as they help destroy mean organisms and bad cells. Problems arise when the body produces too many free radicals in relation to antioxidants. If the free radicals outbalance the antioxidants, the consequence can be chronic inflammation, pain and tiredness".*

For weight hunters and athletes

It is very interesting to understand how breathing affects the metabolism in our bodies, both to be able to lose weight and to find the best fuel during exercise. The more we learn about breathing, we have a greater motivation to practice a Conscious everyday Breathing.

A quote from the book *Conscious Breathing* by Anders Olsson:

> *"Exhaling through the nose leads to a higher pressure in the lungs compared to when breathing through the mouth, which gives better oxygenation. This makes it possible to produce more energy and the muscles can work longer without getting tired. When the access to oxygen is good, more fat can be used as fuel. Better oxygenation also creates more carbon dioxide and less lactic acid. High levels of carbon dioxide build up the pH buffer. A large pH buffer makes it easier to maintain a balance between calcium and magnesium. Lack of calcium and magnesium is closely connected to tight muscles, cramps, twitching and tingling in the legs".*

Stressed, Burnout

Everything that causes stress makes the breathing be faster and/or irregular. We pull up our shoulders, our neck gets tense, we open our mouth so that the breathing cannot happen through the nose. Our fight-flight reaction starts, adrenaline is released which in turn affects the breathing to be faster and the heart rate goes up.

A proper dose of stress can be good, to get things done and react to danger, but what is missing today, is time for recovery in relation to the amount of impressions and activity. A stressed and tense breathing causes oxygen deficiency, which makes the body and brain even more stressed.

I want to thank the writer Anders Olsson with a last quote from his book, *Conscious Breathing*:

> *"To supply the body with oxygen has always been the highest priority. Since we only survive a few minutes without oxygen we need a constant supply of this gas. An impaired breathing leads to an increase in our basic stress, partly because this leads to a reduction in oxygen supply and partly because a greater part of our resources is then needed to supply the body with oxygen. The worse breathing, the higher basic stress, i.e. more mental, emotional and physical stress. On*

the other hand, by improving our breathing we can lower the inner stress and move the opposite direction and increase our physical and mental happiness, ability to concentrate and our feelings of harmony, happiness and satisfaction".

Four good advice

1. Sleep with a sticky tape over your mouth at nights so you in the best and cheapest way get 8-10 hours perfect oxygenation from your body with all its cells.

2. Keep your mouth closed during the day, at work, at home or during your walk/run.

3. Extend the exhalation, which is connected to the body's ability to relax. Think 3-3-3, Breathe in for three seconds, Breathe out for three seconds, and make a pause for three seconds.

4. Join a group for *Conscious Breathing* and give yourself a kickstart with 28 days of breathing practice. There you will get more knowledge about breathing, you'll get motivation and support by us coaches and inspiration to feel and see the progress during the period of change.

Part three

Conscious nutrition

Chapter 8. Food

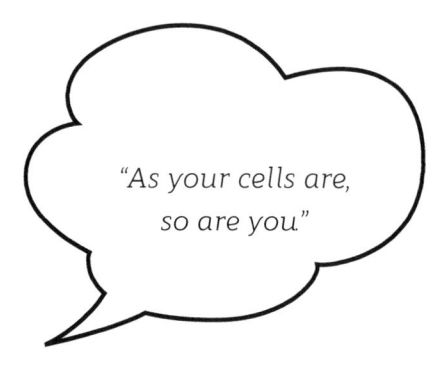

"As your cells are, so are you"

Food for the cells

As I mentioned before, our bodies consist of many billions of cells. For them to be able to do their work, they need energy which comes from the food we eat, and the air that we breathe. The cells get charged by the electrons we get from the ground, all in a complexed process in the mitochondria. I described earlier how we should Ground ourselves and Breathe, to enable the cells to get oxygen and electrons. What I now want to put my finger on, is how we think and act to meet the body's and the cell's need for nutrition based on what we choose to eat. What we put into the mouth is

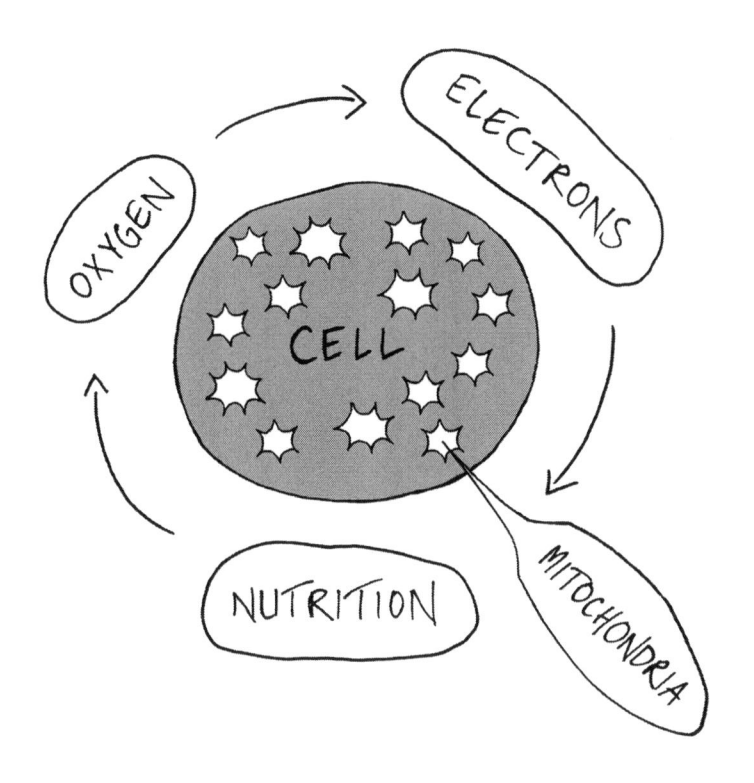

absolutely crucial for which energy, health, vitality, strength and joy we will have. We are all different and our bodies have different needs. No single body has exactly the same need as another body. It depends on our genes, what happened during the pregnancy, during our upbringing and how we ourselves have chosen to maintain our body, our home, our instrument for the soul and the heart. To listen to your own body, to have faith in that we are the captains who are that is making decisions that body, soul and heart are mediating, can be challenging. It is amazing that research today has so many theories around food, how different diets can help different conditions. I have tried several diets because I have been curious about the latest finding on food and health.

The right fatty acid balance – the important foundation for health

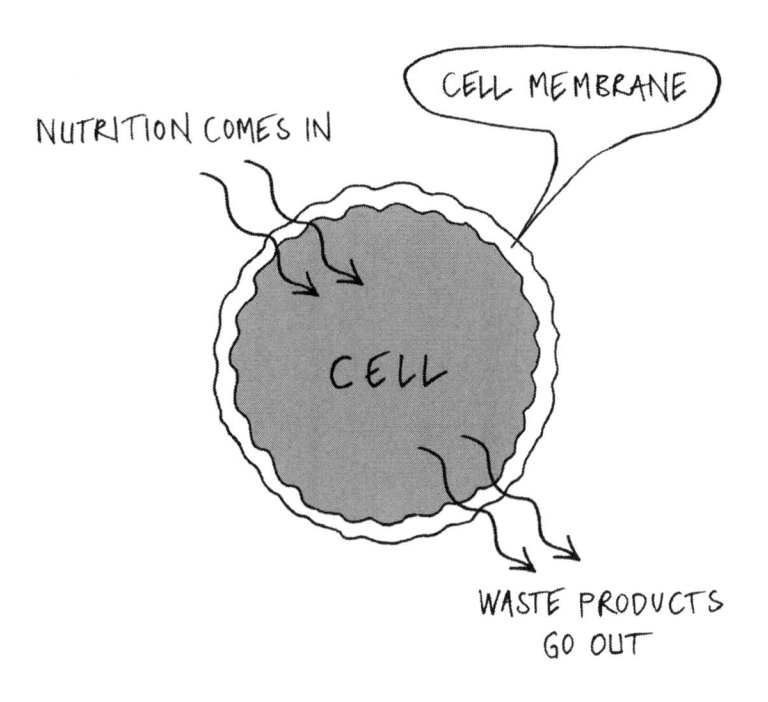

NUTRITION COMES IN

CELL MEMBRANE

CELL

WASTE PRODUCTS GO OUT

Some of the most fundamental for a good health, as I see it, are healthy cell membranes. Around every cell is a membrane, even around the mitochondria. It should be soft, compliant and permeable, to serve as door openers so that nutrition can enter, and waste products can be transported out.

This is achieved when there is fatty acid balance, that is, when there is enough Omega-3 compared to Omega-6 in the membranes. If an imbalance prevails, the membrane becomes stiff and then much of the nutrition bounces towards the membrane and literally goes down into the toilet, without having made any use, which can lead to energy and nutritional deficiency, pain and inflammation.

*"Better soft and compliant
then rigid and impermeable."*

A good balance is max 3 times as much Omega-6 as Omega-3. But in the western world we get between 15 and 45 times as much Omega-6 as Omega-3. This leads to a host of problems ranging from inflammation to concentration difficulties.

In particular, two of the four Omega-3 fatty acids are of importance: EPA (eicosapentaenoic acid) and DHA (docosahexanoic acid). They are essential, which means they are vital. The body itself has little or no opportunity to make it itself. EPA is one of the body's most important stop buttons for inflammation. EPA also lowers elevated blood pressure, increases good, favorable cholesterol (HDL), lowers potentially harmful (LDL) cholesterol, reduces allergic reactions, increases mental function, reduces stress hormones, favors fat burning, discourages depression and mental illness.

DHA is good for heart, eyes and brain, fosters fertility and fetal development. Furthermore, DHA helps people with autism, reading and writing difficulties, ADHD, dyslexia, hyperactivity, difficulty concentrating. It has also been shown to improve conditions in dementia, Alzheimer's, memory disorders, depression and anxiety.

According to researcher Per Kogner, at Karolinska Institutet, those who follow a diet with a lot of Omega-3 are less often affected by cancer. He believes that the Omega-3 fatty acids kills the cancer cells, but protect the normal cells, especially the most sensitive cells of the brain. In this way, the fatty acids become both sword and shield at the same time.

Thomas Seyfried, PhD, a brain cancer researcher, with over 25 years of experience in the field, provided a groundbreaking presentation on cancer at the Ancestral Health Symposium, held at Harvard Law School in 2012. The three main points of his speech were:

- Cancer is not caused by genetic mutations.

- Cancer is a mitochondrial disease.

- Cancer can be treated with ketogenic diets.

Research shows that the mitochondrial DNA can be damaged by carcinogenic radiation, cancerous viruses, carcinogenic toxins and chronic inflammation. Stress decreases with healthy cell membranes.

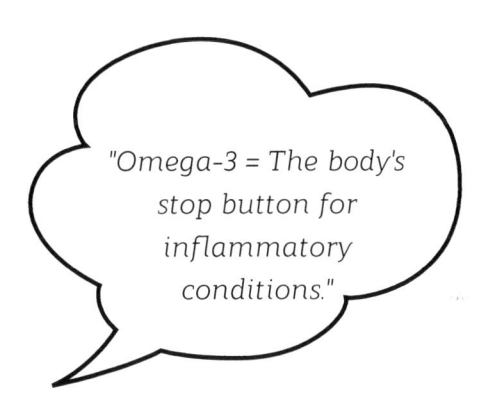

"Omega-3 = The body's stop button for inflammatory conditions."

The fatty acid balance is largely associated with inflammation. Omega-6 is vital and starts the necessary inflammation. Inflammation is thus an important part of the healing process in, for example, adverse diet, tissue damage, smoking, hard training and because of microbes such as bacteria, viruses, fungi, parasites and mold.

Omega-3 should then stop the inflammations, as they are no longer needed. If we have excessive amounts of Omega-6 and too little of Omega-3 in the body, then it will be difficult to put an end to the inflammation.

EPA and DHA are found in oily wild-caught fish and in algae. Mackerel is rich in Omega-3 and if you eat 80 grams of mackerel every day you have filled up your needs. However, you should know that you also get the pollutants to which the fish have been exposed and have stored in the fat.

Vegetable Omega-3 sources such as chia and flaxseed oil, do not contain EPA and DHA but they contain a fatty acid called Alpha Linoleic acid (ALA), good against, among other things, cardiovascular diseases, but they cannot be converted to the valuable fatty acids we get from fatty wild-caught fish and algae. Only 5 % of women and 2 % of men are able to convert ALA to a little EPA and DHA.

However, herbivorous animals can pick up ALA and, in their body, convert it to the right form so if you choose to eat meat you should choose grass-fed meat, that contains larger amounts of Omega-3 than grain-fed animals. The same goes for eggs.

To further help the body reduce inflammation, it is important to review the intake of, for example, sugar, refined carbohydrates and wheat flour. To reduce the amount of Omega-6, it is recommended to reduce the intake of vegetable oils such as sunflower, corn and palm oil, margarine and deep-fried foods. Organic butter, extra virgin olive and coconut oil are preferred instead.

Diseases that usually have their origin in inflammation

Professor, physician and researcher, Karl Arfors has spent the past 45 years devoted to exploring inflammation. He says: "The common denominator of public health is precisely low-grade inflammation". In the journal Medical Access Number 1, 2008, we can read: "Clinical and epidemiological studies have shown that a strong correlation between inflammation and our most common people's diseases – the metabolic syndrome that includes obesity, atherosclerosis, heart attack and stroke, rheumatic diseases, cancer with several other diseases. Progress in basic research has recently put forward strong points that inflammation is a common factor for both initiation and the course of these diseases", writes here Professor Tore Scherstén, Professor Karl Arfors and Associate Professor Ralf Sundberg.

Examples of today's common diseases are cardio-vascular disease, inflammation of the intestine (Crohn's disease, Ulcerative Colitis, IBS,), ADHD, depression, type 2 Diabetes, fibromyalgia, rheumatic disorder, stroke, dementia, psoriasis, schizophrenia, MS, gout, obesity, Guillain-Barré Syndrome, bipolar disorder, epilepsy, migraine, COPD/pulmonary disease, asthma, allergies, eczema and lipedema. The list can be made even longer and as you can see, it applies to both physical and mental states. Many of the above diagnoses we have also been told are chronic.

What does chronic mean?

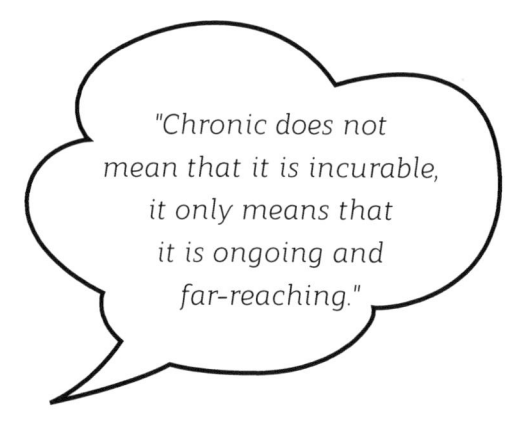

"Chronic does not mean that it is incurable, it only means that it is ongoing and far-reaching."

In other words, this means that we can definitely influence the situation in the direction we desire. Our self-healing mechanisms are amazing if one removes what triggers inflammation and adds to what it reduces.

My own awakening

To understand what prevents inflammation in the body, is a gift and a knowledge I want to share with everyone. I am grateful that my friend and later colleague, Andrea Bodin in Östersund, has given me the knowledge of the fatty acid balance (the ratio of Omega-6 to Omega-3).

As you can see from everything I've tried and the healthy diets I've eaten for a long time, it was incomprehensible to me why my lungs and sinuses remained inflamed. Andrea recommended me to do a fatty acid test. I had no idea that it was possible to see my own fatty acid status through a simple blood test.

We met at home and I did the easy blood test. We put a few drops of my blood on a test strip and it had to dry 10 minutes. Then the blood sample was sent by mail to an independent laboratory in Oslo, from where I get an answer to the body's ability to care for:

1. the body's protection against inflammation

2. the body level of Omega 3 oils

3. fatty acid balance, that is, the value between Omega-6 and Omega-3

4. the mobility of the cell membrane

5. index of mental well-being

After two weeks of impatient waiting, I got the answer. I was so incredibly curious, and I came to find out that I had far too low levels of EPA. It was clear that my body was in a constantly low inflammatory condition. I didn't have a sufficiently strong stop button.

Never before have I been so motivated to take a daily dietary supplement. I took my Balance oil with high-quality Omega-3 every day and looked forward to experiencing the body's response to when the "stop button" would work again.

First, I had a period of deterioration. After a couple of weeks, I got a rash on the face and more mucus in the airways. My shoulder started to hurt again, as when I had a hernia in my neck several years ago. Often, we first get worse, also called cleansing, it occurs when changing diet and lifestyle. Perhaps especially when you give the body what it needs so it can "stand up" and do what it longs for.

This looks different depending on the health status of the person. When the various toxins/body disruptors come out into the bloodstream, the body can be burdened with handling these. This may mean that the immune system becomes a bit more sensitive for a while, so that for example one gets a cold. It can also mean that you can get eczema, because the toxins have to move out somewhere in the body.

If you get worse at first, can also be that the body simply begins to deal with old inflammations that have been simmering. Now they can flare up again to "heal ready" status and the body can be sore/itch/hurt which then can be experienced as if you are getting worse at first.

For me it took a month before I could notice a positive change. Slowly but surely, the yellow/green secretion subsided from the sinuses and the coughing decreased. I fell asleep comfortably in the evening, I slept well and my night sweats disappeared. It was a fantastic feeling to wake up relaxed and rested, as if my body had forgotten how it should really feel.

After 120 days, a new test kit automatically arrived by mail, and it was time to pinch the finger again. The red blood cells had now been replaced and the new test response showed how far I had come towards a good fatty acid balance. For most people who have done the test before and after, the balance is achieved or on a good road to balance, according to the reputable laboratory Vitas AS Norway, which has the world's largest fatty acid balance database.

To keep my good fatty acid balance now, I will continue with the Balance oil daily, until I take my last breath! I am so lucky that I found this simple measure to build long-term health.

But really it is far from a novelty, that our bodies need help to recreate the right balance between Omega-6 and Omega-3. We are many who have heard about Omega-3 and now we are a becoming more and more who understand its important and extensive importance.

My grandfather was a fisherman at Lofoten, in northern Norway, my mother grew up on fish and shellfish from the Helgeland coast in northern Norway and I myself had to endure the intake of fish liver oil during childhood. I wish that as a young adult I understood the importance and continued with the intake for my own health, that I had been dutiful to my own children and I had made sure that they had received their dose of fish oil daily, as of the same importance as having brushed their teeth every day. But unfortunately, I did not have the knowledge and awareness back then to act. I'm truly sorry for that. Forgive me, my beloved children. ♡

The best would have been to act then, the next best thing is to act now. So, from the day I saw my test results, and began to feel how my body responded positively to the Balance oil, I have arranged for my loved ones to get their tests done and their high-grade Omega-3 for breakfast. With the wish that they take them the rest of their lives. Or become fishermen at Lofoten as their grandfather ;)

Choice of Omega-3 Oil

When you are going to choose an Omega-3 oil product there is a few factors you would want to consider to get the full value of the chosen product.

- The dose should be in ratio to your bodyweight, so you can get enough EPA and DHA.

- Your daily intake of EPA should not be less than 800 mg by 50 kg (110 lbs) bodyweight.

- Your daily intake of DHA should not be less than 425 mg by 50 kg (110 lbs) bodyweight, 680 mg by 80 kg (176,6 lbs) bodyweight.

The Omega-3 oil product should have a fat rancidity protection/antioxidant that should keep the product fresh during the whole period of consumption. As soon as the bottle is opened the rancid process starts. The polyphenols in olive oil can handle the strain of the rancidity process very well. The polyphenols protect also us humans when we drink or eat them. They are very strong anti-inflammatory antioxidants and they neutralize the free radicals and other harmful matter.

Why we should take Omega-3?

- Health is determined at the cellular level: Omega-3 gives cells and its mitochondria good conditions.

- It creates healthy cell membranes, and it ensures optimal nutrient uptake and cleansing.

- It reduces the risk of cancer.

- An assurance that you do the most important thing you can, to reduce the risk of our common diseases, physical and psychological.

- If you want to have children – fertility, fetal development and the child's health is greatly affected by the fatty acid balance.

- It restores optimal health.

Examples of clients' positive physical health experiences:

- My skin can handle the sun much better now.

- A friend's tooth stopped burning after seven years, it was inflamed around the nerve.

- My migraines and brain stress decreased, and I was able to return to work.

- My daughter's ADHD and autism changed to calmness, contentment, patience and self-esteem.

Examples of emotional health experiences:

- I recognize myself and my energy/mental strength/creativity.

- The blood test gives a measurable starting position, no one has guessed my health status. Now I feel hope, confidence and motivation to change.

- I am eager to see results 1) to get better health 2) to take the oil consistently every day to do my best for the next test result.

- After 8 years of depression and stress, I can finally sleep.

Some answers to the question "Why don't you want to be without the oil"

- I do not want to take away my hope of recovery.

- I want to live a healthy and long life – I have so much to contribute.

- I reduce concerns about what might otherwise occur.

- I reduce the risk of Alzheimer's as I have bad genes.

- I do not want to lower my immune system from the level it has now.

Advice

- Be prepared for maybe a cleansing reaction, it is a proof that good things are happening. Trust.

- Expect to remind yourself over time, about why you should take the oil. Be sure to be steadfast with your decision just as with toothbrushing.

- Replace these oils: margarine, canola, sunflower oil, corn oil, palm oil with organic butter, extra virgin olive and coconut oil.

- Exclude deep-fried food and store bought cookies.

- Even if your body has the capacity to take care of inflammation better, with fatty acid balance, you need to look at what triggers inflammation, such as gluten, sugar, mold in your house and other factors.

Find out if your "oil lamp" is on red or green!

To get started, contact us in the team!
You find all the contact information at:
consciouslyBarefoot.com

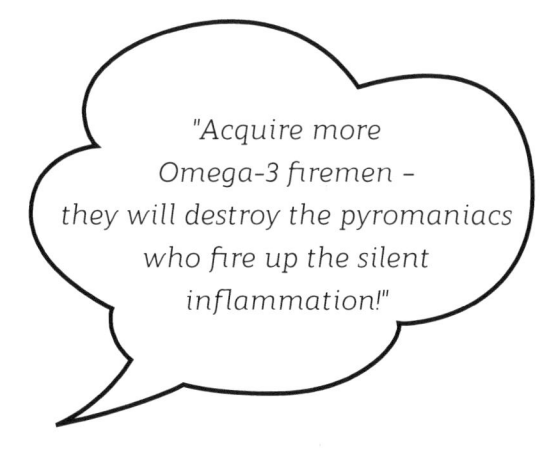

"Acquire more Omega-3 firemen – they will destroy the pyromaniacs who fire up the silent inflammation!"

The ruin of sugar

To describe my own upbringing, the food was based on cereals and white sugar. You know, white bread with butter and jam, to that a cup of tea with three teaspoons of sugar, my mom's homemade "soft cake", with a proper layer of Nutella, and a mug of chocolate milk, that contained around five teaspoons of sugar. I definitely ate eggs, meat, milk and the occasional vegetable from our own farm. But you know how it can be for children; the sweet, white in combination with fat and more sweets, it got to take overhand. And no one put their foot down and said no, enough. My body and my desire for sugar accompanied me as I got older. In fact, even today, I can have a sugar craving that is difficult to control.

Today, there is a completely different knowledge of what our bodies need to grow strong and healthy. And to our great pleasure, the research can now connect how the sugar destroys our immune system, so our bodies cannot protect us against viruses and nasty bacteria. Sugar nourishes the harmful bacteria in the gastrointestinal tract so that the good bacteria succumb, and the harmful ones take over. Today, doctors warn us about the harmful effects of sugar on heart and blood vessels, obesity and type 2 diabetes.

There is an exciting connection between sugar and the fertilization of cancer. To generalize, we can say that all white food is sugar. If we manage to remove the white sugar, white rice, and white flour and other fast carbohydrates, we have taken steps to fight inflammatory diseases. I love to read about the connections in the doctor Giulia Ender's book *Gut*.

I have also met Bitten Jonsson, who is a nurse, educated in the USA, within addiction. She is Sweden's foremost expert on sugar addiction and has published the book *Sugar Bomb 3.0*.

Bitten recommends the book *Why Diets Fail*. Written by Dr. Nicole Avena, the leading sugar researcher right now.

Intestinal bacteria and intestinal flora

Intestinal flora is a living ecosystem which is very sensitive to how we choose to respect and take care of its health. From what we choose to feed the intestinal flora with, it gets the opportunities to either poison us or to take care of us.

The recent years research has given the intestines a totally new meaning. Nowadays the colon and its flora are called our new "super organ".

In the last years there has been a lot of books published on testinal health based on the latest research, and here you can read about different diseases connection to the intestinal flora and how the brain and the colon are connected. It's also points out which diet that gives the best chances to prevent, heal and create an optimal place for the immune system to grow.

Here is a list of some words that are important to know when it comes to intestinal health. You can use them to further research, get more advice, knowledge and recipes on the internet. If you understand the meaning of these words and respect their importance for your body, you will have a wonderful foundation to build your intestinal health and immune defense.

Probiotics - Food or dietary supplements with living good bacteria. Fermented soured vegetables, yoghurt, kimchi, kombucha and water kefir.

Prebiotics - Food for the good bacteria. Water-soluble fibers found in fruit, berries, vegetables and oats.

Inulin – Prebiotics that naturally is found in onions, dandelion greens, rucola, Jerusalem artichoke, red beets, lentils, beans and broccoli.

Resistant starch - Prebiotics that turns to butyric acid in the colon. Exists in boiled cold potatoes, potato starch (2 to 4 tsps. is recommended every day in for example smoothies), green bananas, cashew nuts, raw oats and cooked cold brown rice.

Butyric acid - It has anti inflammatory characteristics. Inhibits growth of hurtful bacteria. Has an effect on the brain and our psychological health.

Vagus nerve – Our important broadband, between the brainstem and the intestines. It links together all the body's organs to the brain and coordinate the body's unconscious and not by will activities like digestion, peristaltic movements and breathing. It regulates our autonomic nervous system, the parasympathetic system.

The vagus nerve is dependent on you eating good healthy food, exercising and avoiding stress.

Wild plants for food, spice and medicine

I love the flavors of wild plants! The original food we had eaten, since we crawled out of the sea and began to munch on what grew around us, how did it taste? Roots, bark, saws, leaves, buds, flowers, fruits, berries and nuts all have their character. Sweet, sour, tender and some are really uncomfortable for our taste buds today.

For me, it is a joy every time, I bring groups into the wild and teach them how we can pick, harvest, eat, or dry the gifts from the forest's large pantry. There is always a wonder about the fresh and crispy flavors that the plants offer us.

It is so powerful when we stop and rest, and then make a wild fire, boil a pot of water on the fire, and then carefully put some eatable leaves in the boiled water, allow the brew to soak for a few minutes and then enjoy, sip by sip, the wild magic drink. It becomes magical because we sit down by the glow of the fire. We take in the greatness of nature. We feel like a part of nature and the food we eat. In the tranquility that arises, we can sense the subtle flavors that the plants offer us. We feel great gratitude for all the beautiful and wild that we can harvest and eat, completely free of charge and natural, as our ancestors did in ancient times.

If you pick and eat wild plants from Mother Nature, that is not near busy roads or other places of toxic emissions, then you have a powerful source of nourishment to your cells. These plants have survived for a long time and have created a vibrant clean energy. They have never been affected by artificial fertilizers or other chemical additives. They are the minerals and vitamins that just that Earth has given them. They are pure nutrition and healing.

Wild plants that can be used as food spice and medicine is a dear subject for me to share. When I guide, I share a booklet with tips and knowledge about each plant, a notebook in which the participants can write down their impressions in their own words. The important thing is that everyone feels confident that the plant that one puts in the mouth is edible. When you are sure of appearance, smell and taste, there is today a lot of information to find online. My own knowledge and experience come from my upbringing in Lapland, near the Pole circle, and from a medicine woman in northern Sweden and Finland that I met over the years. And not least from all the people who walked along on guided tours and shared their memories and knowledge. Often memories like: "Well, now I remember grandmother took broadleaf plantain, (Plantago major), rolled it in her hand until the plant juice came out, then she put it on my laced knee and whip, the next day the wound was healed". Or: "Well, now I understand why Grandfather slept with blueberry branches in his socks!"

Another beautiful aspect of eating wild plants in nature or from your own garden is that the inclination of nurturing and taking care of Mother Earth is increasing. With one's inclination, it becomes a closer relationship and one get more motivated to contribute to a clean and sustainable world without unnecessary emissions and toxins increasing.

Find out your particular nutrition needs

For myself to come to the root with my health problems I was recommended to do a hair analysis. The resulting analysis was to the point, and I was amazed by how it was possible to get all that information by sending a sample of hair to a laboratory. I was so impressed that I chose to do analysis on my closest family with the same exciting results. After some time, I went deeper and educated myself to be a Hair Mineral Analyst. In a quick and professional way, you can discover your current health state and your needs for nutrition, based on how you have eaten, slept, stressed, exercised and have been feeling mentally lately.

What often happens today is that advertising, articles, hearsay or trends make us go to a pharmacy or health food store to buy what we have been "told" should be good. Lots of money is spent on vitamins, minerals and all kinds of dietary supplements that in the worst case deteriorate the body's status. Peter Wilhelmsson, nutritionist (NMTF), naturopath (SNLF) and founder of *Alpha Plus AB* is the person I would like to say is the leading man in Sweden in nutritional medicine today. He introduced functional medicine to Sweden for the first time in 1991. This was done with the help of one of the functional medicine's foremost pioneers, American researcher Dr Jeffrey S. Bland.

Functional medicine is a science-based discipline for evaluating, treating and preventing ill health and promoting health by integrating and focusing on the unique biochemical aspect of each person. This medical model sees the person's lifestyle as the basis for good health, and that lifestyle changes are the basis for better health. Functional medicine represents a well-defined and proven approach and is a diagnostic and treatment system used in functional and integrative medical clinics worldwide.

Do a hair mineral analysis

Minerals and vitamins have been known to be vital components for the body's structure and function, but the interaction between them has proved to be of great importance for optimal health. In collaboration with the laboratory *Trace Element Inc*, USA, you get a multi-page analysis that shows your personal mineral status, advanced analysis interpretation, dietary advice and suggestions for balancing with dietary supplements. It also shows if your body carries any heavy metals that can be damaging to your health. The good thing is that when you get your analysis result, and you know what imbalances your body has, you can now choose to eat what supports, cleans out and builds up based on who you are and what you need.

Linus Pauling, Portland Oregon, who received the Nobel Prize in Chemistry in 1954 and the Nobel Peace Prize in 1962, said: *"You can trace all health problems, ailments and every disease to a mineral deficiency."* He worked as a doctor, researcher, and professor and studied the effect of minerals on the human body and health during many years.

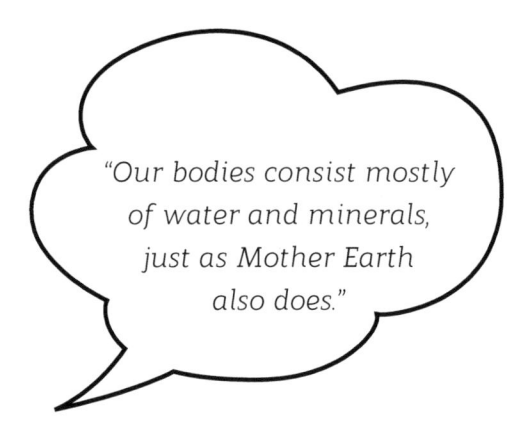

"Our bodies consist mostly of water and minerals, just as Mother Earth also does."

You are your bedrock

One thing that fascinates me a lot is that from the hair analysis we can learn which bedrock dominates the place we live. Up in the inland of the north of Sweden, there are high levels of arsenic in the bedrock. It is a distinctly sparsely populated area and many households have their own water wells. Then it is easy to understand that if you drink a water that comes running in a mountain of arsenic in its constitution, you will drink a water containing arsenic.

In the middle of Sweden, in the area around Jämtland, we have companies that want to explore and extract uranium from our lands. Why just uranium, and why from the beautiful mountainous nature?

Well, because the soil contains high levels of uranium. Since I lived for many years in Jämtland, I have also done a large number of hair analyzes at the people that live there, all with uranium in their bodies. We do not escape the type of bedrock that our food comes from. For better or worse.

Dentists, doctors and therapists worldwide collaborate with Trace Element Inc. in the United States. The company has been around for over thirty years and is the laboratory in the world that I believe has the greatest knowledge and experience in analyzing the connection between the human body and the Earth's minerals and heavy metals.

Diet that suppresses inflammation

During my health journey over the years, I have gained great benefit and pleasure from Karl Hultén's theories and concrete tips on diet for autoimmune diseases and inflammatory conditions. He has a master's degree in biomedicine, and he has researched at the Department of Neuroscience at Karolinska Institutet and has published several interesting books. Karl tells us how healing the Paleo diet can be for our bodies. Paleo, or Stone Age Diet as it is also called, is a way to imitate the diet we humans have eaten since ancient times. The foods we have added in modern times may not always be the best for the body. We have now at the time modern, large-scale agriculture, industrialization and processed food. In the Stone Age, there were small amounts of grains, dairy products, sugar and vegetable oils. What dominated the diet were root vegetables, meat, fish, seafood, vegetables, seeds, nuts and fruits.

It is with great interest that I follow Paleoteket. se, where they step by step address effective methods and give inspiration to reduce symptoms of autoimmune disease and other chronic disorders.

Inflammation Free Diet

IFD stands for Inflammation Free Diet. The IFD theory originated in the United States, created by Monica Reinagel. She has developed a concept that is based on analyzes, made on thousands of foods. Based on about 20 health factors, each food has been studied based, on its chemical composition and content. The issue that is central is whether the food contributes to making human cells stronger, or if it crumbles our cells and thereby breaks us down. Each food analyzed has a numerical value, an IF value. That value tells us about the food depleting the immune system i.e. it is inflammatory, then the value becomes minus, or if the food builds up the health i.e. is anti-inflammatory, then the value becomes plus. For example, a portion of banana has -60 while a portion of kale gets +160, one portion of eggs gets -55, while a portion of the whitefish gets +507 and pike +57. So, I think it is good that in Sweden we have lots of whitefish and pike in our lakes. A fishing rod and a fishing license are all that is needed. In support of finding the right food and score scales, Monica Reinagel has created the app IF Tracker.

IBS free diet without Foodmaps

A few years ago, the doctors thought I should do a gastroscopy to see why I coughed, had heartburn and could not lie on the right side at night without getting cough and burning in the throat. I had it done, and they found that I had a hernia in the stomach. The doctor said that if the problems persisted, I could be operated on, but still he thought I should take medicine. He more than doubled the amount that the health center's doctor had prescribed, as he could prescribe much larger doses. Scary, I thought, and I went home. In my kitchen I happened to come across an article in a little flyer saying, that the dietician at our Health Center was going to start a group for IBS patients (Irritable Bowel Syndrome). I had not heard of the diagnosis, but I thought that it suited me, as the description spoke of, among other things of anxious and bloated stomach, constipation, diarrhea, gasses, stomach cramps etc. The course was inspired by licensed dietician Sofia Antonsson and Jeanette

Steijer, *Belly Balance*. They explain so well how the stomach, brain and intestines interact and effect each other, how stress affects the body and what happens when the food ferments in the stomach.

They advocate that, for some time we should choose a diet free from "Foodmaps" (Fermentable Olig, Di, Monosaccharides and Polyols), i.e. the carbohydrates; fructose, lactose, oligosaccharides and sugar alcohols. Common for these carbohydrates is, that in people with IBS they are poorly absorbent and quick-fermented. Now it is possible to get inspiration and help online at bellybalance.co.uk.

Ketogenic diet

Fast carbohydrates and sugars can cause great damage and inflammation in our bodies, which can lead to many of our welfare diseases such as cardiovascular diseases, joint pain, diabetes, high blood pressure, stomach problems and cancer.

Ketogenic diet was invented in the 1920s. Simply put, one can say that it is a carbohydrate-poor diet, but fat-rich. When I eat a ketogenic diet, my body switches to fuel being driven almost exclusively on fat. My insulin levels become very low and fat burning increases dramatically. My stored fat becomes easily accessible, as a fuel for the body, of course, to great joy for those who want to lose weight, but there are also more benefits. I get less hungry and I get a steady supply of energy from my body fat.

If you want to help heal cancer, it is recommended to eat a strictly ketogenic diet. I myself have tested the diet in a modified variant. I took what I wanted and I let the rest be. For me, for example, it meant that I replaced my regular oatmeal for breakfast to a smoothie cream of a lot of kale, spinach, blueberry, lingonberry, sea buckthorn, olive oil, lemon, boiled cold potato topped with a click of coconut cream. For lunch leek and garlic omelet fried in fat, with lots of salad with olive oil and for dinner, a salad of green leafy vegetables, a small piece of grass fed-based lamb meat, topped with a good oily dressing with olive oil. What happens in my body is that I feel full much longer, when I eat lots of greens and good fats, like olive oil and coconut fat. I get better sharpness in the brain and better endurance. My sources of inspiration are cancer researchers and Professor Thomas Seyfried and Dr. Eric Berg.

The cell's recycling system – autophagy

Fasting is to many people a well-known concept. New research which explains why fasting is so good to strengthen one's health, is done by Yoshinori Oshumi, Japan, receiver of the Nobel Prize in Medicine 2016.

He mapped out and explained how cells that are exposed for starvation, can collect garbage and intruders, and break them down so that new building blocks are created.

Autophagy is a fundamental process for breaking down and recycling of the cells own parts. Auto means self and phagy means self-eating.

Instead of killing the whole cell (apoptosis), some cell parts get replaced. This is the autophagy process, where parts of the cell, old cell membranes and organelles get destroyed and new ones build to replace the old ones. This is a process which is crucial for our whole body. It is important for some diseases like Parkinson's where there are damaged proteins that need to be taken care of.

If the auto function is defect, the nerve cells can't function properly. There might also be strong connections to cancer.

Through the stimulation of autophagy all the untidy proteins and cell parts get cleaned out. At the same time, fasting also stimulates the growth hormone, which tells them to produce new needed parts to the body. We really give our bodies a complete renovating when we are fasting.

The autophagy process helps us to survive when we have been exposed to starvation and other forms of stress. Then we need to break down and reuse the proteins that we already have in the body, so that we fast can rebuild new energy.

By putting stress on the cells and organisms and through lowering our calorie intake one's autophagy starvation increases.

Autophagy is kind of a defense mechanism against aging. If it did not exist, we would grow older faster. It is very popular too look at autophagy in gerontology research, and which role it plays in our aging process.

Fasting gives the best result of autophagy.

Periodic fast means that you consciously exchange between the time window of eating and fasting – the fasting window increases and the eating window decreases. If you eat dinner at 6 pm and breakfast at 10 am, that is 16 hours fasting and 8 hours of eating, 16:8. Water is allowed during the fasting hours.

Already at 12:12 a positive effect can happen, but 14:10 and up is to be preferred.

You do not need to exercise to get a good result of periodic fasting, but the effects seem to be better when it is combined with exercising. You will get the effects of periodic fasting with whatever you eat, but the effects are better with Paleo - or low carbohydrates diet, than traditional diet high in carbohydrates.

Therapeutic fast can be defined a little bit different, but it really takes of when you are without calories in at least 48 hours. The time is a little bit dependent on what you have been eating the days before the fasting begun. The longer you are without calories, the bigger the effects are, and the obvious effects are shown at 3-10 days of fasting. Teas, and liquids made of vegetables are the main nourishments.

Part four

Conscious choices

Chapter 9. Dare to choose your road

"Wouldn't it be nice if ..."

Create new patterns

Isn't it amazing when we decide on a change and then manage to implement it? There are many ways to be inspired to achieve the goals we want. I love the strengthbased approach. Seeing what works and doing more of it. Dream about the desired goal and start creating the stories of how it feels to be already there.

Sometimes it suffices. The thoughts and stories we nourish create our lives. So be careful when you think and talk negatively, and whine, you just create more of the feeling of being a victim. You drain yourself of power, and you create the gloomy life you are choosing to whine about.

Let it go.

How do you want to feel, in let's say a month? What do you want to feel in your body? What do you want your thoughts to be? How do you want to breathe? What do you want to eat? Do you have previous memories of how it felt when you felt that good? Can you remember any occasion when you were satisfied? Take a few moments and feel in your memory and mind, how it was to have the good feeling. Now connect that nice feeling to your dreams about how you will feel about it in a month.

Give yourself the joy of coming back to that feeling several times a day, as you see and feel your new self in front of you

I tell myself: *"It is wonderful to feel and think that: How wonderful it will be in a month when I have stopped coughing and my lungs are completely healthy and strong. I already know, into the smallest cell and mitochondria, the enjoyment and joy how it is to be fully healthy and strong. The quick recovery comes from the fact that I enjoy in the greatest pleasure of walking Barefoot one hour every day, in the morning and in the evening. In addition to that, I get up early and do yoga out on the lawn, to the birds singing their morning songs and I smell the scent of flowers. It is easy to remember to breathe through the nose, deep into the stomach, calm and rhythmic with long exhalation. It makes me so balanced and creative. With these routines I become more harmonious and I make healthy choices for the cells when I cook my meals. I eat lots of organic, locally grown vegetables and wild plants, berries, eggs, Omega-3 /balance oil and add the best fats; organic butter, olive oil and coconut fat. Between meals I drink 2 liters of hot water a day."*

In my life, here and now, everything is perfect and fulfilled!

Help for change

From childhood, we have created the patterns that form the basis of our choices and actions today, for ourselves and others. Many nice and powerful tools are available in our "toolbox". If we look a little closer, we also find patterns, memories, experiences and perhaps trauma that have created sorrow and fear.

There is courage in wanting to become aware of which tools we want to keep and put the focus on, and which patterns we want to develop into something bigger and stronger, so that we can interact with comfort and ease with ourself, our family and others in situations where I more or less reveal my weaker sides.

Many of us share the experience of growing up in more or less dysfunctional families or environments. What do I mean by dysfunctional and who is included in carrying this in their luggage? On one extreme, there are those who have grown up with alcoholism or other addiction problems, such as work, sex, food, religion or other drugs. On the other extreme I ask the question: "Who has not grown up in a dysfunctional environment?" We who have grown up and live in the world today, are affected by consumption, abuse of resources, war, starvation, injustice, individualism and separation. I think we all have patterns within us that we can change. One of the world's largest self-help programs for embracing and transforming old patterns can be found in the 12-step programs.

Feeling of context

If you, like me, like to do things with others, it is a brilliant way to double the power and joy. It may be enough to find just another person you know has the energy and joy you want around you to make you feel that you are growing and being a co-creator of your life, your future and thus becoming part of the solution to one globally healthy world.

Aaron Antonovsky, Professor of Medical Sociology at *Ben Gurion University of the Negev*, Beersheba, Israel, coined the concept of Salutogenesis, which means the origin of health. Antonovsky has meant a lot for a value-based and salutogenic approach. It is about how we can strengthen our sense of context and meaning. The salutogenic approach, focuses on which factors cause and affect health more than the disease itself.

Feeling of context, (KASAM, in English "a Sense of Coherence", SOC) is a concept from the salutogenic theory. According to Antonovsky, an individual can be in good health if he/she can feel involved in a context that is understandable and meaningful. KASAM: comprehensibility, manageability and meaningfulness.

One way for me to incorporate KASAM in my life, has been to drive conversion to a sustainable world from the small and near perspective. I started with myself and then I widened the circles. Then when I understood the context, I took one step at a time, and the spiral of feeling satisfied and happy rotated upwards.

Where can we find a sense of context, how can we satisfy our needs for KASAM?

What will your next step be?

I love to think about which steps we choose to take. Where, in which direction are we going? What imprint do we make? What we take with us from this book, how can it affect which step we will take next? Maybe it will be like this:

CONSCIOUSLY BAREFOOT - We are inspired by this book and get new knowledge about Grounding. It becomes understandable why we should seek contact with Mother Earth. We understand that the radiation we are exposed to daily can be reduced and influenced by ourselves, we handle the situation through new, well-considered choices. It feels meaningful to share the knowledge and vital, to walk Barefoot wherever there is soil, grass, stone or sand for my feet to walk upon, or in the water.

Conscious everyday Breathing - We join a group for 28-day training in Conscious everyday Breathing. There we will be in a context where we deepen the understanding of how extensive breathing affects our lives. It becomes more understandable how Conscious Breathing creates the foundation for health, energy and harmony. Demands on ourselves and training arrangements become manageable, as we do step by step exercises together, and at home. The result of the training will quickly provide benefits for the effort, in the form of reduced feeling of stress, pain and increased vitality. It feels very meaningful to continue deepening the contact with the body and soul through the Conscious Breathing.

Conscious nutrition - We bring the family out in our gardens and start to grow vegetables, or we join a co-cultivation and we pick wild plants in nature. Then we understand where the food comes from, and we understand that we ourselves, can influence the conditions for giving us, and the plants the right nutrition and care. It feels good and manageable to eat healthy food and it makes sense for everyone to help out with sowing, cover cultivation, watering and harvesting.

Conscious choices - I have a dream that together we create a movement forward for increased awareness. Certainly, it would be wonderful if we gave ourselves, each other, everything in nature and Mother Earth unstoppable forces and conditions for love, development and healing?

Ubuntu is a word that inspires. It comes from the Bantu people, one of the largest ethnic groups in Africa. Ubuntu is about being aware of, for example, our thoughts. By focusing positively and consciously on a thought for a few seconds, all other thoughts disappear, and the new thought begins to take shape. The thought gets power from your own energy and your focus. It attracts similar thoughts from your surroundings, your subconscious and your experiences. Then, vivid images of your thought are created in your senses, and a new reality is being created. For every step we take, in the movement with consciously positive choices, the more of the good we attract to humanity. We become involved in actions that brings everything and everyone closer to a healthy Mother Earth.

Can I help you?

Do you long to improve your health?

Do you want your body to respond positively to physical and mental nutrition and stimuli?

Do you need support and power to take the first important steps?

On my website **www.alterskjaer.se** you will find:

Online Training
Lectures
Blood tests/Balance oil
Hair mineral analysis
Air Purifier
Strength-based leadership
Inspiration and research

Thanks

The book you just read really wanted to become reality. My desire to share seasoned with all the "coincidences" that took place during the book's journey from thought to finished book, is something out of the ordinary.

Thanks to all of you who contributed with knowledge, research, positive energy and stimulating issues, friends and all of you that I met when I walked Barefoot in forests, on sports fields and trails.

I would like to send an extra thank you to:

Jenny Holmlund, for making all the illustrations and the book cover, in a way that makes the book take off. ♡

Karin Sundemo, for patiently, professionally and playfully getting the best out of your pictures. Having you behind the camera feels safe. ♡

Andrea Bodin - I have you to thank for my awakening, in terms of the fatty acid balance and its crucial importance for recovery. I am impressed by your solid knowledge and experience of natural health and healing. That you take a stand for reducing the medical care queues, you make sure that knowledge is spread about how inflammation can be stopped. I love you for the woman of action you are. ♡

Göran Gennvi, *Naturakademin Learning Lab*, you are the one who tirelessly demonstrates the benefits of being connected to our inner and outer nature. With you, we can easily immerse ourselves in Conversation on Sustainability to Nature Guest out in the wild. You inspire with your strong energy and your will to contribute to change and the hope for a healthy and brilliant Mother Earth. ♡

The biggest thank you I want to give to my beloved children Sofie, Olle and Liv for being patient "guinea pigs". Thank you for asking curious questions, being suspicious, eager, skeptical and appreciative. ♡

References and research studies

Earthing, Grounding, Breathing and food are part of the new movement for health and well-being, where researchers continuously find new answers and pieces of puzzle that we can benefit from. In the literature and the organizations, I refer to in the book there are lots of research studies to take part of.

I mention a few here:

Part one

From the Earthing institute website "The journal of alternative and complementary medicine"
Volume 22, Number 9, 2016, pp. 757–759
a Mary Ann Liebert, Inc.
DOI: 10.1089/acm.2015.0340
Effects of Grounding on Body Voltage and Current in the Presence of Electromagnetic Fields, Richard Brown, PhD

Is the loss of our planetary electrical roots a factor in the rise of diabetes and other inflammatory diseases that parallels the proliferation of sedentary living and overconsumption of calorie-rich, nutrient-poor food loaded with sugar and high fructose corn syrup (HFC) sweeteners? https://www.earthinginstitute.net/new-hope-for-diabetes/

Intensive care doctors have discovered that grounding may boost the resilience of premature infants and lower the risk of complications. The findings, by researchers at the Pennsylvania State University Children's Hospital Neonatal Intensive Care Unit in Hershey, were published in the journal *Neonatology* in August 2017. https://www.earthinginstitute.net/grounding-help-for-premature-babies/

Dove medical press: "The effects of Grounding (earthing) on inflammation, the immune response, wound healing, and prevention and treatment of chronic inflammatory and autoimmune diseases"

Powerwatch: When it comes to EMF issues, one of the most frequently heard phrases is "There is no evidence to support EMFs having health effects" or simply "There is no conclusive evidence". This is completely wrong; there is an enormous body of evidence out there, but public and even academic awareness seems to be very poor. Therefore, we will be presenting a list of papers and odds ratios which either show serious effects or are considered important papers on the subject which we have collected over the years. This page will be updated regularly.

Part two

From the book *The Power of Your Breath* by Anders Olsson:

Lane N, *Power, Sex, Suicide: Mitochondria and the Meaning of Life*, 2005

Magarian and colleagues, *Hyperventilation syndrome: a diagnosis begging for recognition*, West J Med. 1983 May; 138(5): 733-736

Influence of long-term airflow deprivation on the dimensions of the nasal cavity: a study of laryngectomy patients using acoustic rhinometry, Ear Nose Throat J. 2007 Aug;86(8):488, 490-2

Shturman-Ellestein and colleagues, *The beneficial effect of nasal breathing on exercise-induced bronchoconstriction*, Am Rev Respir Dis. 1978 Jul;118(1):65-73

Part three

Dr. Artemis Simopoulos Center for Genetics, Nutrition and Health has for many years been devoted to research on the fatty acid balance. Here's an example: Dr. Exp Biol Med (Maywood). 2008 Jun;233(6): 674-88. doi: 10.3181/0711-MR-311. Epub 2008 Apr 11. The importance of the Omega-6/Omega-3 fatty acid ratio in cardiovascular disease and other chronic diseases. Simopoulos AP1.

Paleoteket.se - healing diet and lifestyle, Karl and Anna-Maria Hultén talk about the importance of the diet for the body. Here they go through recent research. Karl Hultén is a writer, has a master's degree in biomedicine, has researched at the Department of Neuroscience at the Karolinska Institute.

Certified dietician Sofia Antonsson and Jeanette Steier with the company *Belly Balance* are specialized in IBS. They say on their website: *"The intestinal mucosa from people with the intestinal disease IBS is more permeable to bacteria than healthy bowel, according to a new study led by researchers at LiU".* The study, published in the scientific journal *Gastroenterology*, is the first to be done on IBS with live bacteria. *IBS gut reacts differently to bacteria,* September 5, 2017, Karin Söderlund Leifler.

Mia Lundin highlights research on the benefits of bioidentical hormones: Synthetic progesterone increases the risk of breast cancer while bioidentical progesterone is safe – J Steroid Biochem Mol Biol. Author manuscript; available in PMC 2007 Sep 25. Published in final edited form as: J Steroid Biochem Mol Biol. 2005 Jul; 96(2): 95–108. doi: 10.1016/j.jsbmb.2005.02.014.
Published on the internet: www.ncbi.nlm.nih.gov/pmc/articles/PMC1974841/?report=printable

The connection between different cancers and sugars. A research group at the *Cancer Center at the Beth Israel Diaconis Medical Center* (BIDMC) has investigated the enzyme responsible for the final step in glucose metabolism and has seen the possibility of stopping the growth of tumors as well as reducing established tumors. Lactate metabolism target halts growth in lung cancer model. Study finds that inhibition of lactate enzyme also prevents expansion of aggressive cancer initiating cells. Published on the Internet at: http://www.eurekalert.org/pub_releases/2014-04/bidm-lmt040714.php.

Inspiration

Böcker:

Earthing by Clint Ober, Sthepen T. Sinatra, MD, Martin Zucker

Fats that heal, fats that kill - the complete guide to fats, oils, cholesterol and human health by Udo Erasmus

Nutrition Diva's Secrets for a Healthy Diet, Inflammation Free Diet Plan by Monica Reinagel

One Spirit Medicine by Alberto Villoldo

Out of the fire by Paul Clayton

Paleo Principles by Sarah Ballantyne

The Hormone Balance Cookbook: 60 Anti-inflammatory Recipes to Regulate Hormonal Balance. Lose Weight and Improve Brain Function by Mia Lundin

The New Body Type Guide by Eric Berg, DC

The Paleo Solution by Robb Wolff

The Power of Your Breath by Anders Olsson

Your Personal Paleo Code by Chris Dresser

England:

Powerwatch.com - is used as a forum for a small group of knowledgeable engineers, scientists and medical researchers who are concerned about the consequences of irradiated 'blue world' we are creating. They have been researching the links between electromagnetic fields (EMFs) and health risks for about 30 years and is completely independent of government and industry. We gather information from around the world about EMFs, in order to help the lay person, understand this complex issue. We have designed a number of instruments so that the general public can find out what they are exposed to, and have written numerous publications on the latest research, what is understood and what is not known, and what you can do to minimize any high fields you may be regularly exposed to.

Wikipedia - an encyclopedia with open and free content, developed by volunteer contributors from all over the world. The idea of Wikipedia is possible thanks to a strong belief that people like you and I can work together to build the world's knowledge and make it available and free to everyone, everywhere, thanks to financial support from millions of volunteer donors.

Sweden:

Swedish Radiation Protection Foundation – Everybody is exposed to electromagnetic radiation. There is an urgent need for information and protection – the health of the general public is at risk. *The Swedish Radiation Protection Foundation* works to protect all living matter against harmful EMF exposure.

International:

Bioelecromagnetics Society – acknowledges the importance of student interest in bioelectromagnetic research, they arrange competitions to stimulate exceptional scientific achievements or practical application of electromagnetic fields for human benefits.

---

*"Take what you can use
and leave the rest"*

Twelve Step Program

Printed in Great Britain
by Amazon